Dylan's kiss had heightened her desire, fuelled her passion, until she thought she might spontaneously combust.

Natalie couldn't remember ever feeling so overwhelmed, so out of control. But she was embarrassed, and terrified by how close she'd come to forgetting the difficult lessons of her past. She owed Dylan an explanation but wasn't sure she had one to give. "I'm sorry for letting things get out of hand. We have to work together, Lieutenant."

Dylan held her gaze. "Is that really what's holding you back?"

"No." She smiled wryly. "I don't like to make mistakes."

"What makes you so sure we'd be a mistake?"

"Because I like you, Lieutenant, and I have notoriously bad taste in men."

Available in July 2005 from Silhouette Sensation

Bulletproof Hearts

BRENDA HARLEN

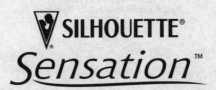

SILHOUETTE®

Sensation™

*First published in Great Britain 2005
Silhouette Books, Eton House, 18-24 Paradise Road,
Richmond, Surrey TW9 1SR*

© Brenda Harlen 2004

ISBN 0 373 27383 5

18-0705

*Printed and bound in Spain
by Litografia Rosés S.A., Barcelona*

BRENDA HARLEN

grew up in a small town surrounded by books and imaginary friends. Although she always dreamed of being a writer, she chose to follow a more traditional career path first. After two years of practising as a lawyer, she gave up her "real" job to be a mum and to try her hand at writing books. Three years, five manuscripts and another baby later, she sold her first book—an RWA Golden Heart Winner—to Silhouette.

Brenda lives in southern Ontario with her real-life husband/hero, two heroes-in-training and two neurotic dogs. She is still surrounded by books ("too many books," according to her children) and imaginary friends, but she also enjoys communicating with "real" people. Readers can contact Brenda by e-mail at brendaharlen@yahoo.com or by post c/o Silhouette Books, 233 Broadway, Suite 1001, New York, NY 10279, USA.

To Stephanie Currie, thanks for sharing your expertise on martinis and medical matters—both of which played an important role in the creation of this story.

To Kevin McCarragher, an artist of a different genre, thanks for your continued encouragement and support over the years.

This book is dedicated to both of you with love and fondest wishes for your very own happily-ever-after.

Chapter 1

A cop shouldn't have dimples.

That was assistant district attorney Natalie Vaughn's first thought when she set eyes on Lieutenant Dylan Creighton in the reception area. She wasn't sure what she'd expected, but it certainly wasn't the more than six feet of trim, hard muscle towering over Molly's desk.

Older, she thought inanely. She'd definitely expected someone older. A grizzled, potbellied cop whose years on the job had made him hard and cynical. It was ridiculous, of course, to make assumptions about anyone. She'd learned long ago that people were rarely who or what they appeared to be.

Dylan Creighton was neither grizzled nor potbellied. And when he smiled at Molly, the D.A.'s secretary, dimples flashed.

Natalie had never been particularly susceptible to dimples. She'd always thought they were boyish, a likely sign of immaturity. But on Lieutenant Creighton, as part of a whole package that could be described as nothing less than mouth-watering, those dimples were devastating.

Thankfully, she wasn't susceptible to dimples *or* men. Not anymore. She'd made enough mistakes in her life as far as the male gender was concerned, and she'd learned her lessons the hard way. She wouldn't forget them just because this man's mere appearance sent her hormones into overdrive.

Still, she'd been so caught up in her perusal she jolted when the phone on her desk buzzed. She forced herself to take a deep calming breath before she picked up the receiver.

"Lieutenant Creighton's here to see you," Molly said.

"Send him in." Natalie was pleased that her voice sounded level, coolly professional. She had no intention of letting the man—or anyone else—know that she was flustered.

She replaced the receiver in the cradle and turned to dig the Merrick file out of the neat stack on the corner of her desk.

The sharp rap of knuckles on glass preceded his entry into her office. Natalie glanced up, a cool but pleasant smile on her lips as she prepared to greet him. She opened her mouth to speak, but her breath caught in her throat.

He filled the small space, his presence overwhelming her. The clean lines of his dark suit couldn't disguise the raw power of his broad shoulders, wide chest and long, lean legs. Mid- to late-thirties, she estimated, with dark—almost black—hair, cut short. His nose was straight, his chin square, his cheekbones chiseled. A real man's man, and every female part of Natalie instinctively responded.

"Dylan Creighton," he said, offering his hand across the scarred wooden desktop.

For a moment, she was too mesmerized by his eyes to respond. She had never before seen such an incredible shade of blue—so deep and dark any woman would gladly drown in them.

Any *other* woman, she amended, and accepted his proffered hand. "Natalie Vaughn."

Still, she could tell that he'd sensed her hesitation. "I'm here to brief you on the Merrick case. I thought you were expecting me."

"Yes. Of course. I just—" wasn't expecting so much of you. "I was working on another file. Preparing for court tomorrow."

"Shouldn't Merrick be your priority?" He was frowning as he folded his arms over his chest. The flex of his biceps—impressive, she had to admit—was evident in the way the material of his jacket stretched tautly over the muscles.

Natalie pushed her hair away from her face and met his gaze evenly. She refused to be intimidated, but she couldn't deny that her heart had skipped a beat. Not because she was afraid, but because she'd wondered—for just half a second— how it might feel to have those arms wrapped around her. And the pang of longing that accompanied the fleeting thought annoyed as much as it surprised her.

"Thanks for your interest in my workload," she said coolly. "But I have four trials next week and Merrick isn't one of them. We don't even pick the jury for his trial until the end of the month."

"If you don't plan on giving this case the attention it deserves, I'm wasting my time here."

"My time's as valuable as yours, Lieutenant, and if you want Mr. Merrick put behind bars—where I fully intend to put him—you'll sit down so we can discuss the case."

Creighton sat, but the scowl on his face only darkened. No sign of those dimples anywhere.

Natalie wasn't sure if she was relieved or disappointed.

"I didn't mean to offend you," he said stiffly. "But the last time we nabbed Merrick, your boss let him walk on a technicality. I don't want to see that happen again."

His criticism put her back up. "I'm aware of the situation, Lieutenant. I'm also aware that there was some question regarding the chain of evidence, which resulted in the charges being dropped.

"Prosecutors are only able to work with the evidence they're given," she reminded him. "As long as the evidence is there, we'll put Roger Merrick away."

"It's Conroy I want," he told her.

The statement, as much as his passionate delivery of it, made her pause. "Conroy?"

He shook his head, as if exasperated by her obvious lack of understanding. "Zane Conroy."

"I know the name," she said icily. "I just don't know why you think this case has anything to do with him."

"Because I know Conroy."

Natalie's smile was as cool as her tone. "And if your apparent familiarity with the man in question was admissible evidence, he would no doubt have been indicted on numerous charges already."

He seemed taken aback by her response at first, then he chuckled. The deep, rich sound of his laughter was both unexpected and unexpectedly warm, and it defused some of the tension that had built between them.

"Okay, I guess I deserved that." He smiled, subjecting her to the full impact of those dimples. "And you deserve an apology."

She sat back, waited.

"I *am* sorry. This case is important to me, and I was annoyed to hear that Beckett had delegated it to…"

"Me?" she supplied.

He smiled again. "Not *you* personally, but to the newest employee in the office."

"Which would be me."

"I thought he would want to handle the case himself."

"Apparently not," she said.

"How old are you, anyway?"

Natalie frowned. "What does my age have to do with anything?"

"How old?" he asked again.

He had no right to ask and she had no obligation to answer. But she understood the importance of picking her battles, and she sensed there could be many of those with Lieutenant Creighton. "Thirty-one."

"You look younger."

"I still don't see the relevance of this."

"It's relevant because I'm trying to figure out why John Beckett would assign a case with such potentially explosive consequences to an attorney who's still wet behind the ears." Then he took the sting out of his words with another of those mind-numbing smiles. "Although they're very cute ears."

Natalie swallowed, unnerved by the unexpected comment. Was the sexier-than-a-GQ-cover-model lieutenant actually flirting with her? If so, she was sure it was nothing personal. He was probably just one of those guys who didn't know how to turn off the charm. That didn't mean she had to succumb to it. Especially not when he'd just questioned her professional competency, albeit in somewhat complimentary terms.

"You're the only one who believes this case is anything more than the routine prosecution of a small-time drug dealer," she told him. "And for your information, I graduated summa cum laude from the University of Chicago Law School five years ago."

"And you've been working as a public defender out of a west-end legal clinic in that city ever since."

She shouldn't have been surprised by his reference to her previous work. It was hardly a secret. But something in his tone, or maybe it was the intense scrutiny of those eyes, made her uneasy. Which only made her all the more determined not to show it.

"What brought you to Fairweather?" he asked.

"I was looking for a change and this job was available."

"You just suddenly decided you'd rather prosecute than defend society's criminal element?"

Despite the casual tone of the question, Natalie got the impression his interest in her response was anything but casual. "*Alleged* criminal element," she said pointedly. "Everyone's innocent until proven guilty."

He laughed again, and Natalie was grateful she was already sitting down, because there was something about that warm chuckle that made her knees weak.

"Somehow I doubt you spouted that line during your interview with the district attorney," he said.

"John Beckett is aware of the work I did in Chicago. In fact, he thought my previous experience made me ideally suited for this position. Who better to anticipate the arguments of a defense attorney than someone who used to be one?"

"I'll reserve judgment on that," Creighton allowed.

"Fine," she said. "In the meantime, maybe you could tell me why you think Roger Merrick will lead you to Zane Conroy."

"What do you know about Conroy?"

"Not a lot," she admitted. And she didn't know if what she'd heard about him was mostly fact or fiction, but his name had been spoken with a reverence usually reserved for the most powerful and dangerous of men.

"Let me enlighten you," Creighton said. "On the surface, he's a respected and respectable businessman. He has several apparently legitimate companies, including a local restaurant and a printing company, but his most successful business is sales."

"Drugs?"

"Mostly. He also deals in weapons and women, and anything else, so long as the price is right. His interests extend from Fairweather to Atlantic City down to Miami and all points in between. With a network like that, there has to be a weak link somewhere."

"And you think it's Merrick."

He nodded.

"Why?"

"Because he's a junkie who deals to support his own habit, and he's terrified by the possibility of spending any amount of time in jail—away from his supply. If we get a conviction on this, he'll give us Conroy."

"Maybe," she allowed. "If he can."

He raised his eyebrows.

"If Conroy's influence is as extensive as you believe, he must inspire a great deal of loyalty—or fear."

"Both," he agreed.

"And it seems unlikely that someone like Merrick—a small-time local dealer—would even have met the man."

"Unlikely," he agreed. "Except that Conroy's younger sister dated Merrick a few years back—a fact which didn't make Conroy any too happy."

"Why did he allow Merrick to continue working for him?"

Creighton shrugged. "Some men will go to extreme lengths to please the women in their lives."

"Are you speaking from experience, Lieutenant?" It was a personal question and certainly not one she'd planned to ask, but it seemed his presence was interfering with the normal functioning of her brain as well as her hormones.

He only smiled again. "I was talking about Conroy—he and his sister are supposedly very close," he explained. "But this is Merrick's second arrest in less than a year, and Conroy has little tolerance for mistakes in his organization. That's why I believe Merrick is the key to bringing him down."

"Then let's get started." Natalie opened the file, eager to focus on something other than the lieutenant's broad shoulders, too-blue eyes and killer smile.

Even if she wasn't susceptible, there was no point in tempting fate.

When Dylan finally left Natalie's office more than an hour later, it was with a grudging respect for the young prosecutor. And she *was* young. Thirty-one years old with five years' experience was too young, too inexperienced, for the job she had to do. Obviously John Beckett thought otherwise, but Dylan wasn't convinced. There was something about her youthful innocence, her freshness and naïveté, that bothered him. Or maybe it was just the woman herself who bothered him.

It had been so long since he'd had any feelings about anything other than the job, he might have laughed at the notion. Except that he couldn't deny the spark of attraction he'd felt—a spark that was as unwelcome and unfamiliar as the heat it kindled inside him. It was more than interest, stronger than attraction. It was desire—pure and simple, and the quick and unexpected punch of it both intrigued and terrified him.

It intrigued him simply because it had been so long since he'd felt such an elemental attraction. And it terrified him for exactly the same reason. More than four years had passed since Beth had been taken from his life, and each day since had stretched like an eternity without her. But now, those four years seemed much too short. He wasn't ready to forget about her, and acknowledging even the stirring of an attraction to another woman seemed like a betrayal of everything they'd shared.

All things considered, it would be best if he could pretend he'd never met Natalie Vaughn. Unfortunately, the nature of their respective jobs necessitated that they'd cross paths and demanded cooperation when they did so.

Which left him trapped in the awkward position between duty and desire. His only hope was to focus on the former and forget the latter. After one meeting with the new A.D.A., he sensed that would be easier said than done.

But Dylan was determined. Since Beth's death, he'd channeled his focus and his passion into his work. He had one reason for getting out of bed every morning: to put Beth's killer behind bars. He didn't intend to let anything—or anyone—interfere with that goal.

In his gut, he knew that the arrest of Roger Merrick was the break he'd been waiting for. Rumors on the street suggested that Merrick had connections that went all the way to the top; connections that could topple Conroy's entire syndicate.

So that would be the focus of his attention, Dylan promised himself as he crossed the parking lot that separated the D.A.'s office from the police station. The very last thing he needed right now was the distraction of a woman, and Natalie Vaughn had "distraction" written all over her in capital letters.

The bullpen was loud, as it always was, the cacophony of sounds both comfortable and familiar. The air was thick with tension and tinged with the scent of bitter coffee. Dylan made his way through the maze of battered desks and ringing telephones to his office. He'd just settled into his chair when Ben Tierney rapped his knuckles against the open door and stepped inside.

"How'd the meeting with the new A.D.A. go?"

"All right." Dylan didn't bother to look up from the report he'd opened, feigning a profound interest in the psychological profile of a serial rapist. He was certainly more interested in the report than in anything the detective had to say.

He'd been partnered with Ben, briefly, several years earlier. Although they'd worked well together, they'd never become friends. When Dylan had been promoted to lieutenant, the other detective hadn't bothered to hide his resentment over his partner being given the job he believed should have been his.

Ben dropped into one of the vacant chairs across from his boss's desk and propped his feet up on the arm of the other. "What did you think of her?"

Dylan bit back a weary sigh and resigned himself to participating in what was sure to be a meaningless conversation. "She seems competent."

"Competent." Ben snorted with laughter. "You're a real piece of work, Creighton. I can think of a lot of words to describe the lovely Ms. Vaughn, and *competent* isn't even one of the top ten."

He shrugged, but he was helpless to banish the image that lingered in his mind. Natalie was an attractive woman. Not beautiful in any traditional sense of the word, but there was something about her that defied description, something that compelled a man to keep looking.

Her hair was a cross between copper and gold, and soft curls of it framed her delicate face and skimmed her shoulders. It wasn't sleekly styled, but sexily disheveled. And she had a habit, he'd realized over the past hour he'd spent with her, of pushing it back off her forehead or tucking it behind an ear when she was concentrating on something.

Her eyes were another mystery—not quite blue, not quite green, but an intriguing blend of the two colors and fringed by long, thick lashes. Her skin was as pale as cream and flawless, save a light dusting of freckles across the bridge of her nose. Her mouth was wide, but balanced somehow by the fullness of her lips. It was an infinitely kissable mouth, and the fact that his mind had made such an assessment only annoyed him further.

"I'm only interested in how well she does her job," Dylan told Ben, wishing it was true. "If we put Merrick behind bars, he'll give us Conroy."

"I wouldn't count on it," Ben said. "Anyone who crosses—or even thinks about crossing—Conroy has a habit of turning up dead."

He shrugged, an acknowledgement of the fact. "He's still our best hope of nailing the big guy."

"Speaking of nailing," Ben continued, waggling his eyebrows. "I wouldn't mind doing some of that with the A.D.A."

Dylan didn't bother to hide his irritation. "Do you ever think of anything but sex?"

Ben grinned. "Not if I can help it."

He shook his head, refusing to admit that he'd had some similar thoughts of his own. At least he had more class than to voice them. Or maybe it was simply unwillingness to admit a resurgence of feelings that had seemed dead for so long.

Besides, he had to work with the A.D.A. on this case, and he had no intention of jeopardizing the prosecution because of his hormones. Of course, if John Beckett was still on the case, he wouldn't need to worry about such things.

"You might try thinking about it sometime," Ben said, pushing away from Dylan's desk. "It might improve your disposition."

"I think I can live with my disposition."

"Maybe you can. But our fair city's newest civil servant might appreciate someone with a little more charm. I think I'll stop by her office and see if she wants some company for dinner." He grinned. "And breakfast."

"Good luck," Dylan said, as if he didn't care one way or the other. But for some inexplicable reason, the thought of Natalie Vaughn with Ben Tierney didn't sit well with him.

Only because he didn't want her attention diverted from

the job at hand, he assured himself. He wanted Roger Merrick and Zane Conroy behind bars for a very long time. He wanted them to pay for what they'd done—for destroying his family.

The ringing of the telephone roused Natalie from her slumber. She'd fallen asleep on top of the covers, the Merrick folder still open on the bed. She blinked, focused bleary eyes on the glowing numbers of the alarm clock beside her.

Twelve-twenty.

She came awake instantly. There was only one reason her phone would be shrilling at this hour: Jack.

Heart in her throat, she scrambled for the receiver. "Hello?"

"Is this the lady from the D.A.'s office?"

It wasn't about her son, then. Natalie breathed a quick sigh of relief. "Yes. Who's this?"

"I've got some information for ya." The voice was masculine, although somewhat high-pitched. Young, she guessed, and nervous. He was talking too fast, his words almost tripping over one another.

"Information about what?" she asked cautiously.

There was a long pause. "I can't talk 'bout it on the phone."

"Talk about what?"

"If ya wanna know, ya hafta meet me."

"I'm not going to meet someone I don't know to discuss something I know nothing about," Natalie said reasonably.

There was a brief hesitation, and when he spoke again his voice had dropped—as if he was afraid someone might overhear him. "I wanna make a deal. Yer the one I need ta deal with."

Roger Merrick, she guessed, glancing at the mug shot stapled to the inside of the file folder. "Roger?"

She heard him suck in a breath, but he neither admitted nor denied his identity. "Do ya wanna deal, or what?"

"If you have information that you think the District Attorney's Office would be interested in, you should discuss it with your lawyer."

His laugh was short, nervous. "Hawkins won't help me."

Natalie frowned, but his response at least confirmed her caller's identity. "I really can't discuss your case without your lawyer present."

"If ya wanna know 'bout Conroy, ya'll meet me."

Natalie felt her blood chill, coursing icily through her veins. She shivered. "Conroy?"

"That's all I gots ta say. If ya want more, come to three-fifty West Fifth Street. Apartment 1D. Come now and come alone."

Then he hung up and Natalie was left staring at the phone, considering the information she'd been given. She knew it wasn't information so much as bait, and she was understandably wary. If Merrick had anything on Conroy, it made sense that he'd discuss it with Hawkins.

But he was hardly the first defendant to refuse to deal through his lawyer. She knew from experience that clients often disregarded explicit instructions given by their lawyers, most often to their detriment. Although she wasn't comfortable with the clandestine meeting, she was even less comfortable with the thought of passing on the opportunity that had been presented to her.

She combed her fingers through her hair, straightened her skirt and reached for her briefcase. And saw the lieutenant's card on top of it.

If Merrick so much as breathes Conroy's name, I want to hear about it.

She hesitated. She didn't want to involve Creighton in this situation. She didn't believe there was any reason to. But the echo of his words in the back of her mind made her pause.

She was under no obligation to apprise him of Merrick's phone call, but she knew he'd be furious if she disregarded his explicit instructions. Reluctantly she picked up the phone and dialed.

She felt a quick tingle of something she chose not to define when she heard his voice on the other end of the line, followed quickly by a pang of disappointment when she realized it wasn't the lieutenant himself but his voice mail message. After a brief hesitation, she left the address given to her.

She doubted that Merrick had any incriminating evidence on Conroy, but she couldn't risk *not* meeting with him. She couldn't pass on the opportunity—unlikely though it seemed—to play a part in bringing the notorious Zane Conroy to justice. This could be her chance to prove herself, to prove to John Beckett that he hadn't made a mistake in hiring her, to prove to Lieutenant Creighton that she was more than capable of handling this assignment.

She drove across town with her doors locked, circled the apartment building at the corner of West Fifth Street three times before finally pulling into a vacant parking spot on the street. Other than the music blaring from an open window several stories up, the street was quiet, deserted and dark.

Three weeks working in the prosecutor's office had opened her eyes to the realities of life in Fairweather. As picturesque as the town was, it wasn't immune to criminal activity, and she had an uneasy sense that she was closer to the hub of it than she wanted to be.

She dialed Lieutenant Creighton's number again, but didn't bother to leave another message when his voice mail picked up.

Her heart was hammering heavily against her ribs. The streetlight at the corner flickered, then plunged into darkness.

Natalie fumbled in her glove compartment for a flashlight. She slid the button to the on position and breathed a sigh of relief when light dispersed from the narrow dome.

Wielding her briefcase in one hand and flashlight in the other, she made her way along the cracked sidewalk with only the meager beam to guide her way. The security door on the rundown building was propped open by a brick, the entrance vestibule smelled of rotting garbage and urine, but a bare hanging bulb provided some illumination.

She tucked her flashlight in her jacket pocket and shifted her case from one clammy hand to the other. Her steps were silent on the threadbare carpet as she made her way down the narrow hall.

Apartment 1D was at the far end, the door slightly ajar. Obviously Roger Merrick was waiting for her.

The muscles in her stomach cramped, her skin tingled with nervous anticipation.

She hesitated outside the door.

This was a bad idea.

A very bad idea.

She started to turn away, chided herself. Maybe it had been a bad idea to come, but she was here now. It would be both stupid and cowardly to leave without at least talking to the man.

She took a deep breath to shore up her courage, and immediately wished she hadn't when a strong, coppery scent invaded her nostrils.

She tapped her knuckles against the door. No response.

She tapped harder, and the door swung back a few more inches. She could hear voices from inside, then canned laughter, and realized it was the television.

"Mr. Merrick?"

Still no response.

He probably couldn't hear her over the sitcom he was watching. Natalie pushed open the door, stepped inside…

And screamed.

Chapter 2

When the shrill beep of his pager sounded, Dylan was watching television—or pretending to, anyway. His feet were propped on the coffee table, a half-empty, forgotten bottle of beer was at his elbow, and his eyes followed the action on the screen while his mind continued to be preoccupied with thoughts of a certain assistant district attorney.

It was a preoccupation that baffled him. Natalie Vaughn wasn't even his type. Not that he had a type, really. He and Beth had started dating when they were teenagers, their friendship developing naturally and comfortably into a love they'd both believed would last forever. Then Beth had died, and Dylan had been alone.

There had been other women since, but none who had ever meant anything more than a way to satisfy his most basic needs. He wasn't proud of that fact, but he was always careful to ensure that those women wanted the same thing he did: simple, no-strings sex.

There was nothing simple about Natalie Vaughn. And after a single encounter in her office, she was haunting his thoughts. The sound of his pager was a welcome interruption of those thoughts.

Fifteen minutes later, he pulled up behind the black and white parked in front of Merrick's apartment building. He nodded to the uniformed officer guarding the door and stepped into the apartment.

Roger Merrick, or what was left of him, was slumped in a chair facing the television. His eyes were open, wide; his chest open even wider. At least three, probably four, shots at fairly close range. A .45 caliber, he guessed, surveying the extent of the damage to the body.

He needn't have worried about rushing over. There was no doubt about it—Merrick was dead. And so was any hope of getting to Conroy through him. He swore under his breath.

It was possible, of course, that Merrick's brutal and untimely end was merely a hazard of his occupation. But in his gut, he knew different. Merrick had possessed information that could have taken down Conroy, and that information was the reason for his murder. *Dammit*.

He scrubbed his hands over his face. Regardless of what the man had done, he hadn't asked to die like this, and now it was Dylan's job to find his killer.

Unfortunately, there wasn't much to be done until the evidence techs had finished with the scene and the ME had examined the body. Detectives Morin and Shepard were already canvassing the neighbors, although in this building, he knew it was unlikely that anyone had seen—or would admit to having seen—anything.

Shaking his head, he turned away from the body.

And saw her.

Fury joined with the frustration pumping through his veins, and he bridged the short distance between the living room and the kitchen in a few quick strides. "What the hell are you doing here?"

Natalie jolted at his question. Her eyes, when they met his, were wide, terrified. Her face was pale, almost white. She blinked, but didn't say anything.

He turned his attention to the techs in the room. "Does the phrase 'secure the premises' mean anything to you people? What the hell is she doing here—other than contaminating a crime scene?"

Out of the corner of his eye, he saw Natalie rise, not quite steadily, to her feet. "I—I called 9-1-1. I f-found him." Her gaze darted back to the body, then quickly away.

Dylan scrubbed his hands over his face again. The absolute last thing he needed right now was the complication of this woman who'd walked out of his unwilling fantasies and into his crime scene. "And how did you happen to find him?"

Her fingers clutched the handle of her briefcase so tightly her knuckles were white. "He c-called me. W-wanted to t-talk. Asked m-me to m-meet him. Here."

He wasn't sure if it was shock or nerves that were causing her to stutter, but obviously she was shaken. Not that he could blame her. He'd seen more than a few nasty scenes in his years with the Fairweather P.D., and this was one ranked right up there with the worst of them. One bullet would have been enough to end Merrick's life. Whoever had pumped those shots into his body hadn't been satisfied with murder, he'd been sending a message.

Dylan filed those thoughts away and forced his attention back to the woman in front of him. She was still dressed in the fancy suit she'd worn at the office earlier—yesterday, he amended. The shadows under her eyes were dark against the paleness of her skin, and she looked as if she was going to topple over in the thin heels she wore.

He grabbed her by the arm and pulled her out of the apartment. The air in the hall, although not exactly fresh, at least didn't carry the stench of violent death. The light was dim, but it seemed that some of the color was slowly returning to her cheeks. "I can't figure out if you're incredibly brave or incredibly stupid. What the hell were you thinking, coming here?"

She straightened her shoulders and met his gaze. Her eyes were focused now, and stormy. "I was doing my job."

Dylan just shook his head. "How long have you been in town?"

"Three weeks," she admitted.

"Well, let me tell you something about Fairweather," he offered. "We don't have a lot of crime, but what we do have mostly originates in this corner of the city."

"I didn't pick the location of the meeting," she snapped back at him.

"But you agreed to meet with him!" He knew he was yelling; he didn't care. He was angry. Furious that his chance to nail Conroy was as dead as the man inside apartment 1D. Even more furious that Natalie had willingly put herself in danger by coming here.

It was a personal reaction rather than a professional one, a natural protective instinct born of growing up with three younger sisters. Three very independent younger sisters who had never appreciated his protectiveness or concern—an experience that should have prepared him for this woman's response to his outburst.

Natalie's own temper worked its way through the numbness of shock that had blanketed her emotions.

"What was I supposed to do?" she challenged. "You're the one who told me that Merrick was the key to getting Conroy. I couldn't ignore his call."

"You should have called me."

"I did," she snapped back.

But Creighton gave no indication of having heard her. "If I'd known he was meeting with you, I would have known he was in danger."

She flinched at the coolly delivered statement, at this confirmation of something she hadn't wanted to consider. She'd had no idea that her brief conversation with Roger Merrick was his death sentence. How could she have known?

But as she'd stood in that room waiting for the police to arrive, staring blindly at his mutilated remains, she'd realized it was something she should have considered. She should have found some way to protect him.

"What did he tell you?" Creighton demanded. "What did he say to get you over here? What information did he have that was worth dying for?"

"He didn't tell me anything," she admitted, some of her anger deflating. She was too tired to stay angry, the situation too futile. "He refused to discuss anything over the phone, insisted that I meet him."

"Someone else was equally insistent that the meeting not take place."

She couldn't respond. There was nothing she could say or do to change what had happened tonight. A man had died— murdered in cold blood—and she couldn't help but feel responsible.

She'd worked murder trials before, from the defense table. She'd detached herself, forced herself to focus on the law rather than the victim, manipulated the facts to her client's advantage. She'd never let herself think about the loss of life, the brutality of the crime. After seeing what had been done to Roger Merrick, she didn't think she'd ever be able to think about anything else.

"Was this your first murder vic?" he asked, a little more gently.

"I've worked homicide cases before," she said defensively.

"So you've read reports and seen photographs," he guessed.

There was no censure in his tone, just compassion and understanding. "Nothing that prepared me for…" She didn't know how to describe the sense of horror that had overwhelmed her when she'd walked into Roger Merrick's apartment and saw what had been done to him.

"Nothing can," he told her.

Natalie nodded.

"Is it safe to assume you've seen more than enough here?" She could only nod again.

"Come on," he said. "I'll buy you a cup of coffee."

Her already unsettled stomach pitched precariously. "Thanks, but I try not to drink coffee at 2:00 a.m.—it keeps me awake."

Creighton smiled at her lame attempt at humor, and—for the second that those dimples flashed—she forgot about the gruesome scene in apartment 1D.

"You were just up close and personal with a dead guy," he reminded her. "I don't think you'll be getting any more sleep tonight."

He was right, of course. But almost as unnerving as the view of what a bullet could do to the human body was Lieutenant Creighton's sudden hint of compassion. "Don't you have to collect evidence or something?"

"The CSU is taking care of that," he told her. "And the ME is ready to take possession of the body."

"Merrick," she said, hating the cold formalities of death that reduced the individual to a designation.

It didn't matter to her that the victim had been an accused drug dealer with a record of arrests longer than her arm, he'd been a person. An hour or so earlier, she'd spoken to him on the phone. He'd been scared when he'd called her. She'd recognized the fear, the apprehension in his voice. Had he known, even then, that his time was running out?

She couldn't help but wonder what might have happened if she hadn't vacillated over her decision to meet with him. "If I'd come right away—"

"You might have ended up like Merrick," Creighton interrupted before she could complete the thought. "Whoever did this to him wouldn't have thought twice about taking out any potential witnesses."

Natalie shuddered. She hadn't allowed herself to consider that possibility, hadn't wanted to admit—even to herself—how foolhardy her actions had been in coming here tonight.

"Coffee?" he offered again.

This time, she drew a deep breath and nodded.

The sign in the window of Sam's Diner advertised breakfast twenty-four hours a day. It was one of the reasons it was such a popular establishment with the local cops.

"Are you hungry?" Dylan asked, sliding into the vinyl booth across from the A.D.A.

Natalie started to shake her head, paused. "I shouldn't be. But I missed dinner, and something smells really good."

"They do a great ham-and-cheese omelet."

"Maybe I'll try it," she agreed, turning over her cup as the waitress approached their table with a pot of coffee in hand.

"Good morning, Sylvia." He greeted the waitress who was already filling their cups.

"Morning, Lieutenant. Ma'am."

Natalie frowned; Dylan grinned. "This is Natalie Vaughn—our newest assistant district attorney," he said.

"Pleasure to meet you, ma'am. Will you be wanting breakfast or just coffee this morning?"

"Breakfast," he answered. "Two ham-and-cheese omelets."

"Can you make mine with egg whites only?" Natalie asked, emptying a creamer into her cup. "And whole-wheat toast, please. No butter."

Sylvia nodded and disappeared back into the kitchen.

Dylan shook his head.

"What?" Natalie demanded.

"It's a greasy spoon. You want to eat healthy, you should go to one of those yuppie delis that serve alfalfa sprouts on everything."

"I like alfalfa sprouts," she told him, sounding just a bit defensive.

"I could have guessed."

"That must be why you're carrying the badge."

He laughed, pleasantly surprised by her bland touch of humor. He'd invited her for coffee because he'd wanted to get her away from Merrick's apartment. He wasn't happy that she'd been at the scene; he was even more unhappy about his fading prospects of apprehending Conroy.

But there was no point in remaining angry with Natalie when Merrick was dead, and nothing to be gained from yelling at her anymore when she looked as if she was beating herself up enough for the both of them. And he had to admire the way she'd held herself together at the scene. He'd have expected her to be crying or throwing up, at the very least cowering.

She'd been shaken, there was no doubt about that. But she'd held her ground and she'd answered his questions, and she'd proven—at least on this matter—that he'd underestimated her.

"Other than tonight, how are you enjoying the new job?" he asked.

The cup Natalie had picked up trembled slightly in her hand. "It hasn't been boring."

"I'll bet you thought you were getting away from the problems of the big city by coming to Fairweather."

"I did," she admitted.

"If it makes you feel any better, this town doesn't have a high rate of violent crime."

"Except in the neighborhood I walked into tonight," she reminded him.

"But still relatively low compared to the bigger cities."

"I'm sure that will help me sleep," she said dryly.

The simple offhand comment brought to mind images of Natalie in bed. In *his* bed. Her sexily tousled hair spread over his pillowcase, her stormy eyes heavy with desire, her lips erotically swollen from his kisses. The image was startlingly vivid, the longing achingly real. "If you're having trouble sleeping, maybe I could help."

Her cup clattered in the saucer as she set it back down, and her eyes were wide and wary as they met his. Obviously his offer had surprised her. No more than it had surprised him.

She cleared her throat. "Are you propositioning me, Lieutenant?"

Was he? If so, that scene in Merrick's apartment must have shaken him more than he realized. He hadn't shared his bed with anyone since Beth died, nor had he wanted to do so. "No." He considered. "Maybe."

Natalie chuckled. The soft sexy sound suited her, he thought. It was as unconsciously seductive as everything else about her.

Sylvia returned from the kitchen with two plates, set them down on the table.

Dylan waited until the waitress was out of earshot before continuing. "What would you say if I were propositioning you?"

"No." Her response was quick and unequivocal.

"Ouch." But he was more relieved than insulted.

She smiled as she toyed with the fried potatoes on her plate. "It's nothing personal. I'm just not in the habit of going to bed with men I've known less than twenty-four hours."

Nor was he in the habit of propositioning women he'd known less than twenty-four hours, but he wasn't going to admit that to her. Acknowledging the uncharacteristic reaction would be too close to acknowledging his feelings—and he wasn't even sure what those feelings were.

Instead, he played it casual. He glanced at his watch. "I'll get back to you later, then."

"Don't bother. I'm also not in the habit of getting involved with people I work with."

"There are always exceptions to a rule."

"Not this one," she said firmly, digging in to her omelet.

He knew she was right. In fact, he'd come to the same conclusion himself—and had promptly forgotten his own resolution the minute she'd sat down across from him.

"Besides," she said, "I find your sudden interest more than a little suspicious when you've made no secret of the fact that you don't approve of my being hired to fill the vacancy in the D.A.'s office."

"It doesn't matter if I approve or disapprove, and I distinctly remember telling you that I was reserving judgment."

"You were quick enough to pass judgment when you found me in Merrick's apartment."

"And I'm not going to apologize for that," he told her. "You shouldn't have been there. However valid your reasons for agreeing to meet with him, you should never have ventured into that neighborhood on your own without telling anyone where you were going."

"I called you," she admitted.

That surprised him. "You did?"

She bit into a piece of toast. Frowned. "It's buttered."

"I'm sure your arteries will survive." He slathered jam onto his own bread. "When did you call me?"

"Before I left to meet with Merrick. I left a message on your voice mail."

"Oh." He usually left his cell phone in the car when he was home. "Why didn't you tell me that earlier?"

She smiled wryly, drawing his attention to the fullness of her soft pink lips. Kissable lips, he thought again. And glistening now with traces of butter. He tore his gaze away, gulped down a mouthful of bitter coffee.

"I tried," she said. "You weren't listening. You just steamrolled past without giving me a chance to explain."

Well, he was paying complete attention to her now, and he wasn't entirely comfortable with the feelings she stirred inside him. Feelings he hadn't been aware of since Beth's death. Feelings he hadn't thought he'd ever experience again. Not with another woman. Grief, guilt and regrets assailed him, not just because of Beth and everything they'd lost, but because he'd treated Natalie unfairly. He hadn't expected the instantaneous attraction, and he'd immediately taken an adversarial stance with her to avoid examining his feelings.

"I guess I should apologize," he said, although she wouldn't know he was referring to more than just his behavior at Merrick's apartment.

She shook her head. "I just want to forget everything that's happened in the past few hours."

"That's not likely. Not once the press starts sniffing around."

She groaned. "I've stepped in it up to my knees, haven't I?"

"Yeah, but you're wearing nice shoes." He'd noticed those immediately. Expensive designer shoes like the ones his sister Hannah favored. With skinny heels that added at least two inches to her height and emphasized her slender ankles and shapely calves. There wasn't much about Natalie Vaughn he hadn't noticed.

She rolled her eyes. "I'm glad you find this amusing."

"In my job, if you don't learn to find the humor in things, you don't last very long."

She pushed her plate aside. "How long have you been a cop?"

"Almost fifteen years." He dumped salt on the potatoes left on her plate, then scooped up a forkful and brought them to his lips.

"You keep eating like that, you won't last another fifteen," she warned him.

He grinned. "It's nice to know that you're worried about me."

"I just hate to think of the loss to the Fairweather P.D. if you die of heart disease."

"Yeah." He put his fork down. "Tierney might get my job."

"I met him yesterday, at the courthouse." She picked up her coffee cup, sipped.

"Then he stopped by your office this afternoon and invited you to dinner."

She frowned. "How did you know that?"

"He told me he was going to."

"Oh."

"Obviously you turned him down."

"I'm working sixteen hours a day, just trying to get up to speed on my files."

"Is that the only reason you declined his invitation?"

"I don't mix business and pleasure," she reminded him. "And even if I wanted to, I don't have time for complications in my life right now."

Dylan didn't think Ben wanted anything more complicated than sex from Natalie, but he wasn't going to tell her that. Not when he had to admit his own thoughts had gone down that same road. "Complications are what make life interesting," he said instead.

"I'll keep that in mind. But I'm a little too tired for a philosophical discussion right now." She pushed her cup aside. "And I should try to catch an hour of sleep before I have to get ready for work."

He nodded. "I'll keep you posted on the Merrick investigation."

"Thanks." She slid out of the booth. "Do me another favor?"

"What's that?"

"Don't tell Detective Tierney I had breakfast with you."

He grinned. It was a tempting thought. "I think I can restrain myself."

"Thanks," she said again.

He watched her walk away, enjoying the subtle sway of her hips in the slim skirt and the flex of finely toned muscles in her calves.

Then he paid the tab and headed out of the diner to return to the scene of the crime.

Chapter 3

Natalie jolted at the quick knock at the door. She'd been jittery all day, unable to banish from her mind the sight of Roger Merrick's bloodied body. Unable to stop thinking about Lieutenant Creighton's reminder that she might easily have met the same fate on her nocturnal adventure.

"I heard you had some excitement last night."

There was no sympathy in John Beckett's clipped tone, nor had she expected any. She'd known this confrontation was inevitable, but her boss had been tied up with jury selection for a conspiracy trial all morning, thus allowing a brief reprieve.

"More than I wanted," she acknowledged, careful to keep her tone light.

"Not even a month on the job and you stumble into the middle of a murder scene. The press is going to have a field day with this," he grumbled.

"It's not like I went out looking to find a dead body," she pointed out.

"You went looking for trouble," he insisted.

"I was in the wrong place at the wrong time."

"Then your being in Roger Merrick's apartment building at 1:00 a.m. was just an unfortunate coincidence?"

"You hired me to do a job," she said. "That's what I was doing."

"Well, you made a mess of it, and you're going to clean it up."

"How?" she asked wearily.

"You can start with the press." He dropped a fistful of pink message slips on her desk.

Natalie swallowed. "What am I supposed to say?"

"Molly is typing up your statement now." He turned toward the door, pausing only long enough to offer a parting shot over his shoulder. "Remember—your position in this office is still a probationary one."

She didn't need the reminder—she was all too aware of how precarious her situation was, how easily her new life could come crashing down around her. Moving to Fairweather had been a big step, one she hadn't taken without careful thought. As much as she'd been desperate to get her son out of the low-income, high-crime neighborhood in which they'd lived, she'd been wary of the offer.

You don't get something for nothing, Shannon had warned.

Her sister was always spouting clichés. "Look before you leap" was another of her favorites.

But in this case, Natalie believed the trade-off was worth it. Getting Jack out of Chicago would be the best thing for him. She'd agreed to let him stay with Shannon until he'd finished out the school year, and to give Natalie a chance to find a home for them. It was all she really wanted—a place where they could both feel settled. And that would happen only if she managed to keep this job.

She shoved the stack of messages aside and buried her face in her hands. She didn't blame her boss for being annoyed. She had overstepped her bounds. Her decision to meet with Roger Merrick had been impulsive and clearly—in retrospect, anyway—unwise. But Beckett had given her the case, and complete discretion to handle it. In fact, he'd seemed more than pleased to get the file off his own desk. If he hadn't thought she was capable of doing the job, why had he given her the case? Why had he ever hired her?

She hadn't gotten any further than these questions when an unfamiliar figure stormed into her office. Natalie hadn't yet had the dubious honor of being introduced to Randolph Hawkins, but she had no doubt that the immaculately dressed man with silver strands woven through dark hair and cold blue eyes glaring angrily across her desk was the infamous defense attorney.

No, *angrily* wasn't an accurate description, she realized. *Dangerously* was much more appropriate.

"You stepped over the line, lady." The words were as sharp and cold as broken glass.

"My name is Natalie. Natalie Vaughn," she told him. "And I'm guessing you're Mr. Hawkins."

"Then you're not a complete imbecile, after all," Hawkins retorted.

Her back stiffened. Regardless of what had happened, he didn't have any cause to treat her with such blatant disrespect. "I understand that you're upset about your client, Mr. Hawkins, but—"

"You knew Roger Merrick was my client?"

"Yes, but—"

"Then why did you attempt to meet with him without my presence?"

"I didn't request the meeting," she said coolly. "Mr. Merrick did. I'm sorry—"

"Sorry?" he snapped. "You should be a damn sight more than sorry. You killed him."

"Now, Randolph," a cool, almost amused voice chided from the doorway. "You know very well that Ms. Vaughn didn't pump those bullets into Merrick's body."

Natalie's gaze flew to the lieutenant leaning casually against the open door. Creighton had been the first in line to chastise her for her actions of the previous evening, so although she was skeptical about his apparent defense she was also grateful for the interruption.

"She signed his death warrant when she agreed to meet with him." Hawkins practically spat the words at Dylan.

"I didn't know he was in danger," Natalie protested.

Hawkins turned back, directing the full force of his anger at her. "Were you also unaware that meeting with a defendant in the absence of his counsel is a violation of both his rights and professional ethics?"

"I told Roger Merrick that I couldn't meet with him without his lawyer," she said.

"And yet you did."

"He was the one who insisted on *not* contacting you."

A brief moment of silence followed her announcement.

"Why was that, do you suppose?" Creighton wondered aloud, pushing away from the door and moving into the room.

"This is none of your damn business, Creighton."

"But it is," the lieutenant assured him. "Murder is very much my business."

Hawkins chose to ignore him. "It doesn't matter what you claim my client said," he told Natalie. "You knew he had counsel, and you had an ethical duty to talk to him through me."

She flinched, because she knew he was right and because it was her determination to prove herself and her eagerness to hear about Conroy that had caused her to overlook that obligation.

But again the lieutenant came unexpectedly to her defense. "You're a fine one to talk about ethics when Zane Conroy has you on retainer."

"Mr. Conroy is a pillar of this community."

Creighton laughed. "If he's the pillar, we're all in trouble."

"In any event," Hawkins continued, "I came here to discuss Roger Merrick, not Mr. Conroy."

He turned his attention back to Natalie. "I'm considering filing a complaint with the state bar association. I'll definitely be making my displeasure known to your boss."

She groaned inwardly, Beckett's reminder of her probationary status fresh in her mind. She'd been on the job only three weeks and she was already in danger of losing it and all her hopes for her and Jack's future along with it. But before she could respond to Hawkins's threat, somehow plead her case, he'd stomped out of her office, the glass rattling in the door as he slammed it behind him.

She sank back into her chair and buried her face in her hands.

"You'd have been prepared for the theatrics if you'd ever seen him in court."

Natalie pushed her hair away from her forehead and forced a smile. "I probably won't be here long enough to have that privilege."

The lieutenant dropped into the chair across from her desk. "He was bluffing."

"Do you think so?" She hoped he was right; she didn't want to start job hunting again.

"Hawkins likes to intimidate."

"He's good at it."

Creighton grinned, flashing those killer dimples and mak-

ing her forget—at least for a second—about her more immediate concerns.

"He won't make any formal complaint about your secret
meeting with his client," he assured her. "If he does, it's bound
to come out that Merrick was the one who requested the meeting *and* the secrecy. It will raise questions about his client's
unwillingness to have counsel present. Which, by the way, is
something you neglected to mention last night."

"I didn't even think about it." She rubbed her fingers over her
forehead, trying to assuage the throbbing ache that had settled
there. "I was thinking about Roger Merrick, not legal ethics."

"Is there anything else you forgot to mention?"

"No." She shook her head. "I don't know." She pushed her
hair back again. "I don't remember what I told you."

"We'll go over it all again some other time. You look ex-
hausted."

She stifled a yawn. "I didn't get much sleep last night." She
shuddered, the image of Merrick's corpse still too vivid in her
mind. "I'm not sure I'll get any more tonight. And I know you
have more questions you need to ask."

"They can wait."

"Why are you being nice to me all of a sudden?"

"I didn't think it was all of a sudden."

She recognized the attempted diversion, but she wouldn't
be diverted. "I've faced a barrage of accusations since my late-
night phone call—the first of them from you. And now you're
the only one who's standing by me."

He shrugged. "You already know how I feel about your visit
to Merrick's apartment. There's no point in rehashing that."

True, but Natalie sensed there was more to it.

"And last night brought back memories," he admitted. "I've
been on the job a long time. So long I'd almost become immune to the horrors of it."

He shook his head. "Not immune, really. I don't think any-one could ever get used to seeing some of the things I've seen. But as a cop, you learn to shut down a little. You have to close off your emotions in order to get the job done."

She'd been in practice long enough to understand what he was saying. As a defense attorney, she'd learned to distance herself from the details to maintain objectivity. She'd trained herself to think, not in terms of guilt or innocence, but in the parameters of the law and the defenses available to her client.

Still, nothing she'd seen as a defense attorney had prepared her for the grisly scene in Roger Merrick's apartment. She shuddered again, unable to prevent the instinctive reaction.

"When I saw you there last night," Creighton continued, "the shock and horror in your eyes, I remembered my first mur-der scene. I couldn't send you away from there on your own."

"Well, thank you. For understanding. For not making me go back to an empty hotel room in the middle of the night."

His gaze sharpened. "Hotel?"

"I've only been in town a few weeks," she reminded him. "I haven't had time to find anything else."

"What hotel?"

"The Courtland. Why?"

He ignored her question to ask another of his own. "Who knows you're staying there?"

She frowned. "My sister. My boss. The hotel staff. Why?"

"Roger Merrick."

She felt the chill crawl over her skin.

"You said he called you," Creighton reminded her.

"H-he did."

"At the hotel?"

She swallowed, nodded.

"How did *he* know you were there?"

"I don't know. I mean, it's not a state secret or anything."

But her flippant response didn't stop the questions that swirled through her mind. How had he known? Could he have followed her after work one night? She wouldn't have realized if he had—she'd never set eyes on him before last night. But if he had, why?

"But it's not common knowledge, is it?" he persisted.

"No," she agreed hesitantly.

He stood abruptly. "I'm going to check into this."

She just nodded and watched silently as he moved to the door Hawkins had slammed shut a short while before.

It was late when Dylan finally left the police station that night. Glancing toward the D.A.'s office, he noticed there was a light on in one of the main-floor offices. Natalie's office.

He paused, car keys in hand. He should go home, cook some dinner, put his feet up on the coffee table, watch a ball game. But his house would be dark, empty.

He glanced toward her office again—watched her silhouette through the window as she pulled her chair away from the desk and sat down. Her hair fell forward to curtain her face as she studied the papers on her desk.

He imagined brushing the hair away from her face, the silky strands sliding through his fingers. He could practically smell the lemony fragrance of her shampoo, the same scent that had brought her image to mind as he'd walked through the produce section of the grocery store earlier.

He turned away from his car and toward the D.A.'s office. If the door was locked, he would go home. He had no reason to interrupt her work.

No reason except that he hadn't stopped thinking about her all day. Even as he reviewed surveillance reports and witness statements, she was there—lingering in the back of his mind, haunting him. There were secrets buried in the stormy depths of her eyes. And scars. He recognized both—not just because he was a cop, but because he had plenty of his own.

He pulled on the handle of the heavy glass door, and it opened.

He thought again of Beth—of everything they'd once shared, everything they'd lost. Because of him. It was his job to serve and protect, yet he'd failed to protect the woman he loved.

His life had changed with her death. He still went through the motions of working and living, but it was as if he existed in an emotional vacuum. Nothing got past the wall he'd erected around his heart—no one had even come close.

Until now.

Which was just one more reason he should stay far away from Natalie Vaughn. He had no interest in opening up his heart again. And he was terrified by the possibility that he might fail someone else.

As he expected, the outer office was deserted, silent. He heard Natalie's voice in the distance, followed the sound toward her office. He could see her through the narrow opening of the door, the receiver of the phone tucked beneath her chin as she typed away at the keyboard of her computer.

"I just have too much work to do." There was an edge of frustration in her voice, as if she'd already made this explanation numerous times. "Please try to understand."

There was a pause as she listened to the response of whoever was on the other end of the phone. She stopped typing and the corners of her mouth curved upward slightly. When she spoke again, her voice was softer. "Me, too. And I'll see you on Friday, Jack. I promise."

Dylan stepped back from the door, trying to interpret what he'd overheard of the conversation. Who was Jack? A friend? A lover? Definitely someone she still had ties to. But if she was involved with someone in Chicago, why would she have moved seven hundred miles away?

And why did the possibility that Natalie was involved with someone else fail to diminish the attraction he felt?

He shook his head, annoyed by the irrationality of his own thoughts. He turned away, determined to walk out the door, away from her. But as he turned, he felt something crunch beneath the heel of his shoe. He winced and glanced down at the offensive instrument—a now broken No.2 pencil.

"Hello?"

He stepped forward, through the door of her office. "It's just me."

"Oh." Natalie frowned, obviously surprised to see him.

"I was leaving the station and saw your light on," he explained. "What are you still doing here?"

She smiled wryly. "I haven't been fired yet."

He chuckled. "I meant, why are you still in your office at seven o'clock on a Tuesday night?"

"Because I have a ton of work to do." She gestured to the stack of files on her desk, sighed. "Since John Beckett has decided not to fire me—at least, not yet—and since I no longer have the Merrick trial at the end of the month, he's given me several more cases to deal with."

"Probably so he could go home early."

"That's the whole point in having subordinates, I guess."

Dylan shook his head. "You know what they say about 'all work and no play'."

"Sure. All work and no play means I'll keep my job another day."

He smiled. "I really don't think Beckett will fire you. Other than your ill-fated decision to visit Merrick's apartment, your work has been exemplary."

"How would you know?"

"It's a small town," he reminded her. "Word travels."

"Thank you, I think."

"Besides, that position was vacant for quite a while," he told her. "If Beckett gets rid of you, he'll just have to advertise and interview for the position again. I can't imagine that's something he'd look forward to."

"I'd like to think that he'll keep me on because of my work, not because it would require too much effort to replace me." She pushed away from the desk and moved to the bookcase to retrieve another text.

She rolled her right shoulder, clearly trying to alleviate the tension. He stepped behind her and laid his hands on her shoulders. She stiffened at the contact, slowly relaxing when his fingers started kneading the tense muscles.

It had been an instinctive gesture, not unlike what he'd have done for one of his sisters. Except that, as soon as he touched her, he realized his mistake. Natalie Vaughn wasn't his sister, and the way his body was responding to hers wasn't remotely brotherly.

She moaned softly, almost inaudibly, but the sensual sound tortured his imagination. Would she moan like that while making love? Would she scream with the pleasure of her release? He focused his gaze on the textbooks, concentrated on reading the titles rather than fantasizing about what he couldn't allow to happen. Objectivity, he reminded himself again.

"I didn't see Richardson in his office," Dylan said, referring to the other A.D.A. Conversation, he decided, would stop her from making those sexy little sounds that were driving him insane.

"Greg's been here longer than I have," she said. "Besides, he has a wife and family to go home to. There's nothing waiting for me in my hotel room except the television."

And a big, wide bed. Which was definitely *not* something he should be thinking about right now.

"If you're going to work late, you should lock the door,"

he advised. "You never know who could walk in." And if she'd locked the door, he wouldn't be here. He wouldn't be touching her, wanting her and torn between longing and guilt.

"I'm waiting for a delivery," she told him.

"Dinner?"

She nodded, evoking mixed feelings of relief and disappointment when she stepped away from him. "Thanks. That feels a lot better now."

Maybe for her. He was definitely feeling a little tense. "What are you having?"

"Kung Pao Chicken."

"Where'd you order from?"

"The Golden Dragon."

Dylan grimaced.

"Bad choice?"

"Not the best," he agreed.

Natalie sighed. "It's one of the things I already miss about Chicago—knowing where to get the best takeout."

One of the things. Was Jack another? He wasn't going to speculate; he wasn't going to ask.

"Don't you cook?" he asked instead.

"Not if I don't have to," she admitted. "Do you?"

"All the time."

"Really?" She sounded shocked.

"Is that so hard to believe?"

"Yes. Are you any good?"

He grinned. "I've been told my marinara sauce is to die for."

"Marinara sauce, hmm?" She sounded interested, almost in spite of herself.

"I also make a great meat loaf."

"And you're still single?"

He felt a pang, sharp and swift, but gone as quickly as it had come. Maybe too quickly. That was something he'd have to think about later. Now he shrugged. "You want to skip the Kung Pao Chicken for a home-cooked meal?"

"It's tempting," she told him, "but I've already ordered, and I really do have a ton of work still to do."

"Maybe some other time?"

"Maybe," she agreed vaguely.

It wasn't an outright refusal, anyway. He decided to quit while he was ahead. "I'll let you get back to work," he said. "Make sure you lock up behind the delivery man."

Dylan's instincts had always been good. Of course, fifteen years on the force had taught him a lot about people and helped him to hone his natural intuition. But he was still undecided about the new assistant district attorney.

Were his hormones confusing the issue?

Possibly.

Probably.

He couldn't deny that he was attracted to her. She was an attractive woman, and he was a fully functioning man with all the normal impulses. But he had no intention of acting on those impulses.

Despite his clumsy overtures, he kept his personal life separate from his job—no exceptions. To cross that line would hamper his objectivity, and without objectivity he couldn't be a good cop. Dylan had always prided himself on being a very good cop. It was more than his job, it was his identity. And it was all he had left.

So he wasn't happy that thoughts of Natalie Vaughn occupied an inordinate amount of his time. Of course, it didn't help that she'd walked into the middle of a murder scene and thus firmly planted herself in one of his cases.

The investigation of which was proving to be surprisingly fruitful in the early stages. A .45 caliber pistol had been found hidden behind a bush outside Merrick's apartment. Preliminary reports showed no prints on the gun, which wasn't surprising. But the fact that the serial number on the weapon had been filed down gave him hope. It was unlikely the perp would have bothered with such a task unless the weapon was registered in his name. Or maybe he got the gun from someone else who'd used it for illegal purposes. In either case, once the lab guys retrieved the number, the police would have—if not the killer—at least a starting point in their search for whoever had pulled the trigger.

While awaiting the results from the lab, he had other avenues of investigation to follow—and one of those led him to Natalie's hotel room.

She answered the door wearing her pajamas.

Silk, he guessed, based on the way the dark green fabric shimmered and molded to her curves. A deep V-neck revealed a tantalizing glimpse of cleavage and a simple gold heart on a delicate chain resting against her creamy skin.

He forced his gaze upward, noted that her eyes were more green than blue tonight, and shadowed with fatigue. Her face was bare of makeup, those full, lush lips unsmiling.

"What are you doing here, Lieutenant?"

"I needed to ask you some more questions about what happened the night of Merrick's murder."

She sighed. "I was really hoping to get some sleep tonight."

"It won't take long," he promised.

She stepped away from the door to allow him to enter.

He took a quick survey of the room. The wallpaper was cream-colored with wide gold stripes, the carpet deep and plush, the furniture made of glossy cherry wood. Tasteful, classy. Of course, the Courtland Hotels had a reputation for luxurious accommodations and exceptional service—and a five-star price tag. Obviously the new A.D.A. was being well paid.

The queen-size bed was still made, although the spread was slightly rumpled and there were files and notes scattered on top. The television was on, but the volume was low. A small desk was in front of the window, a battered leather briefcase open on top of it. A single glass of red wine sat on the table beside the bed, half-empty.

"Can I get you a drink?"

He shook his head.

Natalie perched on the edge of the bed, gestured for him to take a seat.

He remained standing.

She picked up her glass, sipped.

"Were you drinking that night?"

"Do you disapprove of my having a glass or two of wine, Lieutenant?"

"I simply asked a question."

"No, I wasn't drinking that night," she told him. "I'm only drinking tonight because I'm hoping that a few drinks might help me forget what I saw in Merrick's apartments at least long enough to get some sleep."

"It won't," he told her. It was always difficult to face death—violent death was the worst. The scene in Merrick's apartment would have made a lasting impression on anyone, and he knew it would be a long time before Natalie would sleep without being haunted by dreams of what she'd seen. The realization stirred his compassion. "I wish I could tell you the memory will fade, but some memories never do. You just have to learn to live with them."

"Do you?" she asked. "Learn to live with them, I mean?"

"There's nothing else you can do," he told her. What he *wanted* to do was to offer comfort and understanding. He knew how hard it was to face the darkness alone, and he wished he could spare her that.

Objectivity, he reminded himself, and took a mental step back.

"All right. Let's get through your questions."

He pulled the chair from behind the desk and straddled it, facing her. "What time did you receive the phone call?"

"Twelve-twenty."

"You're sure about that?"

She nodded. "I'd fallen asleep. The first thing I did when I heard the phone ringing was look at the clock."

"Did the caller identify himself?"

"Didn't we cover all this already?"

"I want to go over it again, to make sure we haven't missed anything."

She sighed.

"Did the caller identify himself?" he asked again.

"Not right away."

"But he did give you his name?" Dylan prompted.

She paused, frowning. "No."

"Then why did you assume it was Roger Merrick?"

"Because he talked about making a deal, and when I said he should talk to his lawyer, he said Hawkins couldn't help him. I guessed his identity, and when I called him by name, he didn't deny it."

"But he didn't confirm it, either."

Her frown deepened. "No."

"How did you know where to find him?"

"He gave me the address and I scribbled it down while I was on the phone with him." She rose and moved toward the desk, her knee brushing against his thigh. Silk against denim, yet the brief contact sparked like flint on steel.

She froze, her wary gaze locking with his for just a second. But in that brief moment of connection, he saw it in her eyes: awareness, attraction. Then she turned away, rustled through her briefcase.

Dylan had to remind himself to breathe, to remember the purpose for his visit. He was here to do his job—it was his only hope of getting justice for Beth.

She handed him a single page with the hotel insignia at the top. He gave it only a cursory glance.

"That's the address he gave me," she told him.

"The address *the caller* gave you," he amended.

"That's what I said." She picked up her glass again, her fingers trembling slightly. Was she shaken by their brief contact—or was her nervousness a result of the topic of their conversation?

It didn't matter—he was here to investigate Merrick, not the A.D.A. The reminder didn't cool his hormones, but it at least focused his thoughts. "What if I told you that Roger Merrick didn't make that phone call?"

"But—but I spoke to him."

"Had you ever spoken to him before?"

Natalie shook her head. "Why would I?"

He ignored her question to ask another of his own. "How long did it take you to get to Merrick's apartment after you left here?"

"I don't know," she admitted. "I don't remember."

"Approximately?"

She shrugged. "Twenty minutes. Maybe half an hour."

He'd followed the route earlier that evening. It had taken twenty-two minutes to drive from the hotel parking lot to the front door of Merrick's apartment building.

"Did you leave your room as soon as you got off the phone?"

"No." She studied the contents of her glass rather than

meeting his gaze. "I tried calling you first. And when I didn't get an answer…"

She hesitated, and he thought he saw a touch of color rise in her cheeks.

"When I stopped to think about it, I wasn't thrilled about the idea of driving across town at that time of night on my own," she admitted. "It took me a few minutes to talk myself into it."

The embarrassment, the hint of vulnerability, made him want to reach out to her, to offer comfort and reassurance. But he wasn't her friend, he was a cop—and he needed to act like a cop. "A few minutes—five? Ten?"

"Maybe ten."

"Which would put you at his apartment by one o'clock?"

"I guess so."

He nodded. He'd been paged about fifteen minutes later, which corroborated her version of events. Almost.

He folded his arms over the back of the chair, his eyes locked on her. "I just don't understand why Merrick would ask you to meet him on the other side of town if he was already here."

Natalie frowned. "What do you mean?"

"We checked the hotel's phone records," he told her.

"And?"

"The call that came into this room was made from one of the courtesy phones in the lobby."

Chapter 4

Natalie shook her head, refused to believe it.

"Not only that," Creighton continued, oblivious to the effect his words had on her. "But preliminary reports from the ME indicate that Merrick was killed sometime between 10:00 and 11:00 p.m. In any event, he was dead before you received that call."

"Th-that's not possible."

"Science doesn't lie," he said.

It took a minute for the implications of what he was saying to sink in. She drew in a deep breath, determined not to reveal the hurt. "And if science doesn't lie, you think I am."

"I don't disregard any possibility."

She pushed her hair away from her face and realized her hand was trembling. She curled her fingers into a fist to hide this evidence of weakness. She was *not* weak. She was upset and tired, and she'd been ambushed in her own hotel room.

But the mental reassurance did little to calm her quivering nerves.

If what he said was true, who had made that phone call? Why? And why did he think she was lying?

"What possible reason could I have to lie about this?"

He shrugged. "People lie to the police all the time."

"I'm not 'people,'" she said coolly. "I'm an assistant district attorney. We're on the same side."

"Are we?"

She felt her heart sink. After his actions in her office the other day, she'd begun to think he might be an ally. Her mistake. Again. "What are you implying, Lieutenant?"

"I'm not implying anything," he denied. "I just want to make sure I have all the facts straight in this investigation."

"Then why are you badgering me instead of investigating?"

"Because you've somehow ended up in the middle of this damn case."

"Not by choice."

Creighton was silent for a long moment. "Willingly or not," he finally conceded, "you've been drawn into it. Why?"

"How should I know? It's not like I *wanted* to walk into that apartment and find a dead body." She shuddered as the image of that brutalized body flashed in her mind again. Far worse than the sight was the smell that continued to haunt her—the sickly sweet scent of violent death and fresh blood.

"Someone wanted you to," he said. "That's the only other reason I can think of for that phone call you received."

"Or maybe the ME miscalculated. Maybe it really was Roger Merrick who called, and maybe he really wanted to give me information in exchange for a deal."

"Merrick didn't make that phone call."

Natalie stood up, crossed over to the window. It had started to rain, and the heavy drops lashed ferociously against the window, streaking down the cold glass like angry tears. A flash of lightning briefly illuminated the inky sky.

She hated storms, always had, but she'd learned the only way to overcome her fears was to face them. She continued to stare into the darkness of the night as the low rumble of thunder sounded somewhere in the distance.

More unnerving even than the threat of the storm were the implications of Creighton's assertion. She didn't want to believe him. She didn't want to consider that anyone other than Merrick had made that phone call, because if she did, she'd have to consider why. And she didn't like any of the possibilities.

"I don't even know anyone in this town," she said softly. "Why me?"

"That's what I'm trying to figure out," he told her.

She nodded. As much as she wanted to stay angry with him—to have a target for the frustration inside her—she knew it wasn't his fault. She only wished he'd give her the same consideration.

She continued to stare out the window. The rain continued to batter at the glass. She wished Jack was here. She wanted nothing more than to put her arms around him and hold him close. She wanted—needed—the comfort only the presence of her child could give.

But Jack was in Chicago, and she was here, alone. So incredibly alone.

Unbidden, tears sprang to her eyes. She blinked fiercely, determined not to yield to the array of emotions overwhelming her. Shannon had always accused her of being too emotional. Natalie couldn't deny it was true. Nor could she deny that following her heart had only led to misery. But she'd learned her lesson, and if she couldn't always control her feelings, at least she'd learned to harness them. She wasn't going to yield to them now.

Despite this assertion, a single tear slipped free, tracked slowly down her cheek. She brushed it away impatiently.

"Natalie?"

She started. His voice was close, too close, behind her. More startling than his proximity was the realization that this was the first time he'd ever spoken her name. And in that low husky tone, the single word sounded incredibly intimate.

Then he touched her. Just a hand on her shoulder, but the simple gesture of comfort completely obliterated her defenses.

"I didn't mean to come down on you so hard," he said gruffly.

She just shrugged, her throat too tight to speak.

"I'm trying to say I'm sorry."

She nodded.

Dissatisfied with this nonverbal response, he settled both his hands on her shoulders and turned her around to face him. She was too close to the edge, too close to losing the control she prized so highly, so she kept her head averted, the fall of hair curtaining her face.

It was a mistake to believe he'd respect such a physical barrier. If she'd learned anything about Lieutenant Creighton in the past couple of days, it was that he could be relentless. She'd forgotten that he could also be considerate, as when he'd taken her for breakfast rather than sending her away from the murder scene alone. And when he'd come to her defense against Randolph Hawkins.

He was both relentless and gentle now, the finger under her chin forcing her head up, the eyes that met hers filled with compassion. "I am sorry."

Two more tears slid down her cheeks. Very gently, he brushed them away. Natalie blinked, startled by the tenderness of the gesture, alarmed by the undeniable urge to lean into him, to seek shelter in his strength. She didn't want or need his comfort. She didn't need anything from any man.

But she couldn't pull away. The intensity of his gaze held her immobile. She'd never seen eyes so dark, so warm, so achingly blue. He took a step closer. Their bodies weren't quite touching, but she could feel the heat emanating from him and the awareness that crackled in the air between them.

As impossible as it seemed, his eyes grew even darker. She recognized his desire, it was echoed in her own heart. But she couldn't acknowledge it, couldn't respond to it. Giving in to the inexplicable attraction she felt for this man would be more dangerous than walking into the electrical storm outside with a lightning rod.

But the logic of her mind was silenced by the yearning of her heart. When his gaze dropped to her mouth, her lips tingled with wanting. He tilted his head toward her, and she felt her blood pulse slow and heavy through her veins. She couldn't breathe, couldn't think. She could only want. And she desperately wanted his kiss.

The sudden and unexpected crack outside the window made her jump. It also snapped the thread of tension that seemed to have woven around the lieutenant and herself, allowing her to breathe once again and to fully appreciate the recklessness of what she'd almost allowed to happen.

"It's just thunder," he said soothingly, reaching for her again.

The reasonableness of his tone infuriated her almost as much as the childishness of her own reaction. "I know it's just thunder," she snapped back. "I just don't like storms very much."

She turned away and wrenched the curtains across the window. If only she could shut away her emotions as easily.

At least the booming intrusion had reminded her of the situation, of her need for self-preservation. She didn't want to let this cop get close, to resurrect feelings she'd long since buried. Creighton, however, didn't appear to be giving her any choice in the matter. That realization, more than anything else, fortified her defenses. She wasn't going to be any man's pawn.

"I wasn't making fun of you, Natalie." His tone was still patient, understanding. "Everyone has fears."

"Forget it," she said stiffly. "I'm not usually this thin-skinned—it's just been a rough couple of days."

"I'd say that's an understatement."

She shrugged again. "I'll feel better after a good night's sleep."

"Maybe," he acknowledged. "But I don't think you'll get it here."

She frowned. "Why not?"

"Because whoever placed that phone call knows you're here," Dylan reminded her.

"You said the call was made from the lobby. Whoever called was in the hotel, not in my room."

"If he got that far, it's not a stretch to think he could go farther."

"This is a reputable hotel with good security. If someone is determined to find me, I don't see how I'll be safer anywhere else."

"You could register at another hotel under a false name."

"I'm not going into hiding."

"You could be in danger, Natalie."

He was doing it again—using her given name, implying a camaraderie she didn't want, wasn't willing to acknowledge. "Make up your mind, Lieutenant. One minute you're practically accusing me of working with the bad guys—the next, you're suggesting I'm their target."

"I know you're not involved—" He broke off abruptly. "Dammit, I *don't* know you're not involved. I don't know you, or anything about you. And I've been a cop long enough to know that prematurely ruling out any possibility is dangerous."

Well, that clearly set the battle lines again. She felt an uncomfortable sinking sensation in the pit of her stomach, a sense of loss she didn't understand.

Creighton drew a deep breath, raked a hand through his already unruly hair. "But I don't believe you're involved. I saw you in Merrick's apartment. I know how that scene affected you. You wouldn't have reacted that way if you'd had any part in making it happen."

She didn't know why his statement filled her with such relief. It shouldn't matter to her what he thought, but for some inexplicable reason it did. Determined to ignore her internal response, she tried a wry smile. "Then I should be grateful I have a weak stomach?"

"You should be cautious."

"I am," she told him. "And right now I'm tired. Can we table this conversation to a later date so I can get some sleep tonight?"

He hesitated, as if he intended to pursue the topic further, but then he nodded. "All right." He took a business card out of his pocket and held it toward her.

"You already gave me one," she reminded him.

"This one has my home number on it. If you can't get me on my cell, try me there."

"I don't think—"

"Use it," he said, placing the card in her hand. "Anytime."

But Natalie wouldn't call, and Dylan knew it.

He knew it when he left her hotel room, and he was even more sure of it the following morning when he selected the dumbbells for his biceps curls. He often started his day with a workout as he found physical exertion usually helped clear his mind. Of course, he usually started his day with more than three hours of sleep. And he usually *didn't* have a woman lurking in the back of his mind.

No matter how hard he tried to banish Natalie from his thoughts, he couldn't stop thinking about her. He couldn't stop wondering why her apparent uninterest bothered him so much.

He dropped the dumbbells back into the rack and moved to the leg press.

Because she wasn't uninterested, dammit. He'd felt the crackle of awareness between them in that hotel room. He'd seen the flare of desire in the stormy depths of her blue-green eyes as he'd lowered his head to kiss her. And he'd seen, just as visibly, how she'd shut her emotions away and distanced herself from him.

He should be grateful she'd had the sense to back away from a potentially volatile situation. A situation that he'd created despite the knowledge that any kind of personal relationship between them was a bad idea. But he wasn't feeling grateful, only annoyed and incredibly frustrated.

He adjusted the weight on the machine and began his repetitions with a vengeance.

"Someone's in a mood this morning."

Dylan glanced up at Joel Logan, a local private investigator and longtime friend. "I haven't seen you around here in a while," he said, opting to ignore Joel's comment.

"I'm a newlywed," his friend reminded him. "I've found more enjoyable forms of exercise to start my day."

He deliberately let the weights slam together again.

"Tough case you're working on?"

"Not really."

"Then what's put you in such a mood?"

"There's nothing wrong with my mood," Dylan denied.

Joel shrugged and sat down at the rowing machine. "If you don't want to talk about it, just say you don't want to talk about it."

He started to say just that, changed his mind. He *did* want to talk about it. More, he *needed* to talk about it. And Joel was just the person to talk to. "What do you know about the new A.D.A.?"

Joel eased back, released the handles. "Natalie Vaughn?"

He nodded.

"Not a lot," his friend admitted. "Only that she moved here from Chicago to fill the vacant position. And, according to the papers, she's a witness to the murder of a drug dealer."

"She didn't actually see the murder. She found the body."

"And?"

He hesitated. He'd started this conversation because he knew he lacked objectivity where Natalie was concerned and he wanted someone else's opinion. But now that he had Joel's attention, he was reluctant to voice his concerns. Reluctant to admit aloud how preoccupied he'd become with the new A.D.A.

"I'm not sure," Dylan admitted. "There's something about this case, the way it's unfolding and her part in it, that's bothering me."

"Or maybe it's just the new A.D.A. who's bothering you?"

He wanted to deny it, but he knew his friend would see right through him. Not only was Joel a P.I., he used to be a cop—and a damn good one, too. Any denial would only lead to more questions, so he opted for diversion instead. "The murder vic—the drug dealer—worked for Conroy."

All trace of amusement fled from Joel's face. He rubbed a hand unconsciously over his abdomen, over the scar from the bullet one of Conroy's thugs had plugged into him several years earlier. "Can you prove it?"

"I thought I could."

"Maybe Conroy thought you could, too. Maybe that's why Merrick's dead."

Dylan nodded. "That's what I figured."

"But?"

"But I don't understand where Natalie fits in."

"Natalie?"

He cursed himself for the slip. "Vaughn," he clarified. "The A.D.A."

Joel looked as though he wanted to comment further, but he let it pass, focusing instead on the investigation. "Why does Natalie—" he grinned "—have to fit in?"

"It wasn't a coincidence that she found Merrick's body. Someone called her, pretending to be Merrick. Someone deliberately set her up to find him dead."

"Sounds like something Conroy would do—manipulating her, testing her."

"But why?"

Joel shrugged. "To see how she responds. To see if she might challenge him. Because he's a sick bastard."

Dylan couldn't deny any of those possibilities. "I don't like it. And I don't understand why a young, apparently bright attorney would give up a burgeoning career to move more than seven hundred miles away. To Fairweather, no less."

"You think she must have some ulterior motive for settling in our fair city?"

"You can't already have forgotten about Warren Blake," he chided.

"No," Joel agreed. "But just because the former A.D.A. had an agenda doesn't mean Natalie Vaughn does."

"It doesn't mean she doesn't, either."

"Do you really believe she's on a mission? Or are you afraid of the way you feel about her?"

He scowled. "I don't know what you're talking about."

"It's pretty obvious that Ms. Vaughn has got under your skin, and you don't know what to do about it."

"No one has gotten under my skin."

"Then why are you asking me these questions? Why aren't you doing your own detective work to get the answers you want?"

"Because I'm not sure it would be ethical for me to investigate her background when I have to work with her."

"Or because you'd feel guilty for taking subversive action when your interest is personal."

"Bull."

"If you want my advice," Joel told him. "Don't do it. Don't go digging for answers that she'd probably provide if you just bothered to ask. That's a mistake I made with Riane, and I wasn't sure she'd ever forgive me for the deception."

"This is hardly the same situation," he said. "You were in love with Riane."

"Not at first. And I had all kinds of excuses and justifications for what I was doing, but what it came down to in the end was that she'd trusted me and I'd let her down."

"I just need to know that she is who she says she is."

"Do you have any reason to believe she's not?"

Certain details nagged at the back of his mind: the fancy hotel room, the designer clothes. She certainly didn't fit the image of an overworked and underpaid civil servant. But his suspicion was just that, with nothing of substance to back him up. Not yet, anyway. "No," he said at last.

"Then let it go."

Dylan nodded his agreement, but he wasn't sure he could.

When she'd accepted the job in Fairweather, Natalie thought she'd planned for all contingencies. She hadn't anticipated the complication of Lieutenant Creighton. Maybe she should have, but it had been so long since she'd felt anything for any man. After her disastrous relationship with Jack's father, she'd concentrated on two things: her son and her career. She'd dated little, and only when social obligations warranted. She was too busy raising a boy to even think about a relationship with a man.

Until Dylan Creighton walked into her office.

He was the first man in more than seven years to pique her curiosity, stir her hormones.

Stir? The man had simply touched her last night—nothing more than his hands on her shoulders—and she'd practically been reduced to a quivering mass of need. The fact that he apparently reciprocated her feelings only made them that much more difficult to ignore.

Still, she was confident that he'd soon lose interest. In her experience, men lived for the chase, but without encouragement, they quickly grew tired or moved on to other prey.

All she had to do was keep their relationship strictly professional and he would move on. Besides, he was probably only interested because she was new in town and he'd already conquered all the natives. Well, Natalie had no intention of being the latest in what was undoubtedly a long list of conquests. She had no intention of being conquered by any man.

Wednesday night, Natalie realized she'd made a mistake in underestimating the sexy police lieutenant. It seemed as if every time she turned around, she was running into the man she most wanted to avoid.

This time it was at Carla's Pizzeria.

She was walking out as he was coming in, and the easy grin he gave her completely melted her bones. Damn, but he should be required to have a license for that smile—and those dimples were positively lethal.

She tried to pass, but he remained in the doorway, unapologetically blocking her route. "That's a big pizza," he commented.

She shrugged. "Take-out special."

"What are you going to do with it?"

"Nothing illegal," she assured him, shifting the large square box.

He grinned again, and her knees nearly buckled.

"Are you sharing it with anyone?" he asked.

"I don't know many people in this town, and I don't know anyone else who likes anchovies on their pizza."

"You know me, and I like anchovies."

"You're kidding."

He shook his head. "And I can't imagine you'll be able to finish all that by yourself."

"Leftovers are good for breakfast," she told him.

"You'd eat pizza for breakfast?"

"Why not?"

He just shook his head again. "Share your pizza with me and I'll buy you a box of cereal," he offered.

Natalie wasn't sure it was a good idea to spend any more time than she had to with Lieutenant Creighton. She was sure it was a *bad* idea to invite him to her hotel. "Why aren't you utilizing your alleged culinary expertise to prepare your own dinner tonight?"

"It's not nearly as much fun cooking for one."

Somehow, she didn't think he'd have any difficulty finding a dinner companion, if that was really what he wanted.

"It's not a lot of fun eating pizza alone, either," he said.

"Eating is a necessity, not a form of entertainment."

"Do you have some moral objection to sharing conversation with a meal?"

"Not generally," she allowed.

"Just tonight—or just with me?"

"Look, Lieutenant, it's nothing personal, but—"

"Isn't it?" he interrupted.

She didn't, couldn't, respond.

"I have cold beer in my fridge."

She didn't imagine that his home would be any safer than her room. But she knew she couldn't continue to refuse without seeming completely antisocial, or without causing the lieutenant to speculate on her reasons for refusal. If he ever figured out how attracted she was to him, she could be in real trouble.

"And I thought you might be interested in hearing about the progress we've made in the Merrick investigation."

As if he didn't know that was an offer she wouldn't refuse. "All right."

He grinned, and the reappearance of those dimples reminded her that this was a very bad idea.

"Your place or mine?" he asked.

She was a firm believer in the home-turf advantage, but at present her home turf was dominated by a bed. "Yours."

The aromas of basil and garlic teased Dylan's taste buds when Natalie opened the lid of the flat cardboard box. His mouth began to water in anticipation as he pulled plates and napkins from the cupboard.

"Smells good." He peeked over her shoulder at a pizza loaded with toppings—pepperoni, sausage, mushrooms, peppers, olives, anchovies.

But suddenly all he could smell was the fragrance of her shampoo, and all he really wanted was a taste of her.

He backed away quickly.

What had he been thinking when he'd invited her into his home? He'd thought it was fate when he'd walked into the pizzeria as Natalie was walking out. Prior to that, the night had yawned ahead of him like a huge void. He'd just wanted company—something to alleviate the emptiness of his evening, the emptiness of his life. Or so he'd convinced himself.

Now that she was here, he realized he'd been wrong. He didn't want company—he wanted Natalie.

He turned his attention to the contents of the refrigerator, reminding himself of all the reasons any personal involvement between them would be a mistake. But he was starting to think it might be worth the risk. "Beer, wine or soda?"

"Beer's fine," she said.

He grabbed a couple of bottles from the top shelf, twisted off the caps before setting them on the table.

"Dig in," he said.

She helped herself to a slice, the cheese dripping down the sides, toppings sliding away with it. "I assume Carla's was a good choice if you were planning to get your dinner there, too."

"The best pizza in town."

Reassured, Natalie bit into her slice.

Dylan tried to concentrate on his own pizza, but he was preoccupied with thoughts of the woman sitting across from him. His feelings were still unclear, her reasons for coming to Fairweather still suspect. But he couldn't deny the attraction he felt, an attraction that grew stronger every time he saw her. An attraction that was undoubtedly hampering his objectivity as far as she was concerned.

"How was youth court today?" It was a neutral topic of conversation, a reminder of their professional relationship. A desperate attempt to keep his attention away from the low neckline of the soft blue top she was wearing. A top that clung enticingly to the gentle curve of her breasts.

"Slow. We had covered everything on the docket before lunch."

"This isn't Chicago," he reminded her.

She raised her bottle of beer in a toasting gesture, the movement causing the low neckline of the shirt to dip a little lower. Low enough that he caught a glimpse of shadowy cleavage.

"Hear, hear."

He forced his gaze upward again, just in time to see her tip the bottle to her lips, to watch the seductive movement of her throat as she swallowed.

Chicago, he reminded himself. They were talking about Chicago—and it was the perfect opening to pry just a little. "Did you hate it that much?"

She shrugged, as if she'd already revealed more than she wanted to. "I didn't hate it," she denied. "There just weren't many opportunities for me there."

"What kind of opportunities?" What had drawn her away from the city? What could she possibly find in Fairweather that she couldn't find in Chicago?

"Job prospects, primarily."

"But you had a job."

She nodded, and surprised him by admitting, "That I *did* hate."

"Why?"

"Because it seemed so meaningless." She selected another slice of pizza from the box, frowned. "I believe that everyone is innocent until proven guilty. I believe every accused person has the right to counsel. But after a while, the ideals aren't so ideal anymore."

"Was there any one case in particular that disillusioned you?"

She shook her head. "I just got tired of defending the same clients month after month, on the same or similar charges, listening to their pathetic excuses and justifications for breaking the law, and having to turn those explanations into a viable defense."

"Burnout," he concluded.

She considered, shrugged. "Maybe."

"You were looking for a career change." He could understand that. "Why Fairweather?"

"Because I really wanted to go to Sacramento," she told him, "but I'm not licensed to practice law in California."

Dylan grinned. "Pennsylvania's a close second to the capital of the Golden State?"

"Maybe not close," she allowed. "But if you're still thinking that I have some ulterior motive for coming to Fairweather, you're going to be disappointed. I was looking for a new job, and there was one available here. It was that simple."

He still wasn't convinced of that fact. He also knew she wasn't going to tell him any more than what she already had. But there was one more question he had to ask, one more thing he needed to know. "Any personal ties back in Chicago?"

She froze in the act of peeling a slice of pepperoni off her pizza. "What do you mean?"

"Boyfriend? Fiancé? Husband?"

"No. To all of the above. And no again."

He frowned. He'd wanted to ask about the mysterious "Jack," but the last part of her response sidetracked him. "What was the last 'no'?"

"Not interested."

Chapter 5

Dylan was tempted to pursue the topic, tempted to see if he could prove her wrong. Now that he knew she wasn't involved with anyone else, there was no reason not to see where things might go between them. Except that their working relationship complicated the situation. And even if they didn't have to work together, he wasn't sure he was ready to face the depth of the attraction he felt for her—or if he ever would be.

So instead of tempting fate, he lifted another slice of pizza from the box.

"You promised me an update on the Merrick case," she reminded him.

"There's not a lot to tell. Although the lab techs did manage to get a serial number off the gun they found in the bushes outside of Merrick's window."

She plucked an olive off her pizza, popped it in her mouth. "I thought it had been filed down."

"They use a special kind of acid that acts on the stamped metal to lift the number, allowing us to trace the weapon," he explained. "Some more sophisticated criminals actually gouge into the weapon with chisels or drills to obliterate any trace of the manufacturer's mark."

"Which means you've got an amateur assassin—or someone who wanted the gun to be traced."

He nodded, impressed by her insight and logic.

"Who did the gun belong to?"

"The registered owner is a man by the name of Ellis Todd, an accountant at Denby & Witter."

"You don't sound very encouraged," she said. "Don't you believe CPAs can be criminals?"

"Of course they can," he agreed. "And I'd be knocking on his door right now if the charge was embezzlement or tax evasion. But ballistics hasn't concluded that the discarded gun is the murder weapon."

"They can't prove it, or they haven't finished the testing?"

"They haven't finished the testing."

"What's the next step then?" she asked.

"I'll talk to Todd, see if I can shake anything out of him. But I'm not optimistic."

"If you can imagine this man guilty of other charges, why is murder so unbelievable?"

"Not unbelievable, just unlikely. There's no apparent connection between Merrick and Ellis."

"What kind of connection were you hoping for?"

"Something. *Any*thing." He took a long swallow of beer. "Like maybe Merrick had been banging Ellis's wife—" he broke off, glanced at Natalie apologetically.

She shook her head. "You'd like Ellis better as a suspect if his wife was unfaithful?"

"I'd understand," he clarified, helping himself to the last slice of pizza.

She rolled her eyes. "Last time I checked, infidelity wasn't a valid criminal defense."

"Not a defense—a motive."

"Ahh. You're looking for a crime of passion."

He couldn't help the slow smile that curved his lips, couldn't ignore the opening she'd given him. "Aren't we all looking for passion?"

He watched as the gentle teasing in her eyes faded to wary awareness before she dropped her gaze. She reached for a napkin and concentrated on wiping her fingertips, deliberately avoiding further eye contact. "Some of us are just looking to do our jobs."

"Is that really all you want, Natalie?"

She crumpled the napkin and nodded, still refusing to look at him.

"Passion doesn't intrigue you?" he persisted.

"Passion terrifies me," she admitted, and despite the patent absurdity of the statement, he sensed it was the truth.

"Why?"

"Because it makes people do things they wouldn't otherwise do."

"Like commit murder?"

She managed a small smile and finally glanced at him. "Sometimes the consequences are a little less extreme," she acknowledged. "But there are always consequences."

Her words confirmed what he'd already suspected: someone had really hurt her. What he hadn't suspected was the deep and primitive urge that stirred inside him—an urge to find the man who'd done so and make him pay.

"Bottom line," Dylan said, forcing his attention back to the topic at hand, "is that I'll be talking to Mr. Todd in the very near future, but I'm not hoping for much."

"Are there any other leads?"

"Not at this point. Although I'm still optimistic that we'll turn up something, somewhere, that will lead us to Conroy."

"Is it true…about the videotapes?"

His gaze sharpened. "Where did you hear about those?"

"Greg Richardson."

"What did he tell you?"

"That Conroy likes to have tapes made of the executions he orders, apparently for his own viewing pleasure."

"That's the rumor," he agreed. "Although others believe the purpose of the videos is to ensure the continued cooperation of his employees."

"What do you think?" she asked. "Do the tapes even exist?"

He thought of Joel Logan, of the bullet his friend had taken in the gut, of the videotapes that had been in his hand when he'd gone down. Videos that had never been found.

"Yeah." He nodded. "They exist."

She shuddered at the thought, and Dylan decided it was an appropriate time to change the subject.

"Do you like baseball?" he asked.

She seemed surprised by the abrupt question, and a little wary. "Cubs or Sox?"

"How about the Phillies and the Mets? The game's on TV tonight. Stay and watch it with me."

"Why?"

His smile was wry. "Because I spend far too many nights sitting home alone."

The simple honesty of the statement destroyed Natalie's resolve.

She really should go—for so many reasons, not the least of which was the growing attraction she felt for the lieutenant. Leaving was smart, and for the past seven years, she'd made a concerted effort to do the smart thing, to evaluate all possibilities and the consequences of each. Tonight, for just this once, she wanted to disregard logic and reason. Tonight, she didn't want to sit in her hotel room alone.

She felt comfortable with Creighton, more comfortable than she'd expected to feel. Somehow, between their first meeting in her office and breakfast at Sam's Diner, their mutual mistrust had dissipated—or at least been set aside. Since then, she'd realized that she genuinely liked the lieutenant.

He was dedicated. She'd never known anyone so devoted to the quest for truth and justice. He was understanding and compassionate, strong yet gentle. And despite the hazards of his job, he'd retained a sense of humor. He laughed and he made her laugh, and it had been a long time since she'd had anything to laugh about.

It was this liking, far more than the attraction she felt for him, that worried her.

"Will you stay?" he asked again. "For a while?"

No. She definitely had to go. But she said, "For a while."

The warmth in his smile convinced her that she'd done the right thing in accepting his invitation. And if her heart started to beat just a little bit faster, well, that was something she would deal with.

He pushed back his chair, scooping up the pizza box and their empty bottles. "Do you want another beer?"

Did she need alcohol fogging her brain when he did that so effectively himself? "No, thanks."

"Soda?"

"Sure."

He grabbed another beer for himself, handed her a can of ginger ale. She followed him into the living room, trying not to stare at his butt. But he really did have a great back end. And incredible shoulders. And dimples to die for.

He bent to retrieve the remote control from the coffee table, drawing her attention back to his derriere. She forced herself to move past him.

He didn't take the other end of the sofa, as she'd expected, but sat in the middle. Close enough that she could see the faint white line of a scar in the dark stubble on his chin.

A remnant from childhood? Or a hazard of the job?

She didn't ask. She didn't want to talk about his past or her own. It would be wiser—and safer—to keep their relationship strictly professional. If only she could stop thinking about how it would feel to have those muscular arms wrapped around her, those tempting lips against hers, the hard body pressing into her own.

She put the can to her lips and drank, hoping the bubbly liquid would help cool the heat suddenly coursing through her veins.

"Are you married?" The words blurted out of her mouth without any warning.

Creighton looked startled. She couldn't blame him. She'd been no more prepared for the question than he, and heat immediately flooded her cheeks.

His smile was slow, devastatingly sexy. "I thought you weren't interested."

She shrugged. "Not interested doesn't mean not curious."

He held her gaze for a long moment, and she felt as though she could gladly drown in the depths of those blue eyes. The baseball game continued to play out on the television. Somewhere in the distance sounded the crack of a bat, the roar of a crowd. She was aware of nothing but the man beside her.

"No," he said at last. "I'm not married."

"Girlfriend?"

His eyes remained steady. "No."

She nodded.

"Does that satisfy your…curiosity?"

His words were teasing, but the atmosphere was suddenly charged with tension, sizzling with awareness.

She wasn't sure she could speak, so she nodded again.

"Good."

He leaned closer, slowly lowering his head toward her.

She knew he was going to kiss her.

She knew she should stop him.

Then his lips brushed against hers, softly, slowly. It was a feather-light touch, more of a caress than a kiss.

His eyes were still open, still locked with hers. She saw heat and hunger, felt both escalating inside herself.

Boundaries, she reminded herself.

Then he kissed her again, and the boundaries crumbled.

He lingered this time, his mouth warm and firm. She offered no resistance, felt none in her heart. She wanted this— so much more than she knew she should. But for now, she just wanted.

Want yielded to need. Fierce, driving need. The bold, erotic stroke of his tongue had her lips parting instinctively, opening for him. She tasted the tangy sauce of the pizza, the yeasty essence of beer, and a deeper, more potent flavor that she knew was uniquely his.

She couldn't have said how it happened. She didn't know whether he lifted her or if she crawled, but somehow she ended up on his lap, her knees straddling his hips. He slid his hands beneath the hem of her sweater, grazing the bare skin of her lower back with his fingertips. His touch was unbelievably gentle, unbearably exciting.

His fingers skimmed upward, tracing the line of her spine. She shivered, the subtle movement causing her nipples to graze his chest. She gasped with shock, with pleasure, as spears of fiery heat arrowed from the peaks to the pit of her belly. All the while, he continued to kiss her.

His hands moved lower again, then over her ribs, his thumbs brushing against the undersides of her breasts. Her nipples were already tight, aching. She sighed softly, urging his continued exploration, and moaned when he caressed the swollen tips.

Instinctively, her hips tilted forward, seeking—and finding—the evidence of his arousal. She wriggled, positioning the weight of his erection against the soft juncture between her thighs. This time it was Dylan who moaned.

His lips skimmed down the column of her throat; his whiskers scraped her tender skin. He nipped and soothed, teased and tantalized. Every kiss heightened her desire, every touch fueled her passion, until she felt as though she might spontaneously combust.

Natalie couldn't ever remember feeling so overwhelmed by sensation, so completely out of control. No one had ever made her feel this way. Not even Eric—

She froze, the heat that had been coursing through her body supplanted by an ominous chill. She pushed away from him, scrambled to her feet. She turned her back, but she could still feel his eyes on her as she straightened her sweater.

"Natalie?"

She was embarrassed and ashamed by what she had allowed to happen between them, terrified by how close she'd come to forgetting the difficult lessons of her past and frustrated by the unsatisfied yearning inside. She drew in a deep, steadying breath. She owed him an explanation, but she wasn't sure she had one to give.

"Hey." He stepped in front of her, cupped her cheek gently.

She prepared herself to face his irritation, his anger. She knew he had every right to be annoyed by her hasty withdrawal. When she forced herself to meet his gaze, she saw only concern and compassion. Somehow, that made her feel worse.

"I'm sorry."

"For what?"

"For letting things get out of hand, for letting you think…" Her words trailed off.

"I wasn't thinking anything. I was just enjoying the moment." He held her gaze. "I thought you were, too."

She was, which only made this more difficult. "We have to work together, Lieutenant."

"Is that really what's holding you back?"

"Yes." She sighed. "No."

He frowned, clearly waiting for her to explain this cryptic response.

"Our working relationship complicates the situation, but it isn't the only reason this can't happen."

"What's the real reason?"

She smiled wryly. "I don't like to make mistakes."

"What makes you so sure we'd be a mistake?"

"Because I like you, Lieutenant, and I have notoriously bad taste in men."

He chuckled softly. "I think I'll choose to be flattered rather than insulted by that remark."

"I'm not trying to flatter or insult you. I'm just being honest."

"Are you?"

"Yes."

"Then tell me you don't feel the chemistry whenever we're in the same room together."

She couldn't lie to him, wouldn't lie to herself. But in the interest of self-preservation, she chose to downplay the situation. "Chemistry is overrated."

He skimmed a finger down her cheek. She shivered instinctively in response to the lazy caress, proving his point. She couldn't deny that she reacted to his touch, but she refused to give him the satisfaction of pulling away.

"I still have work to do tonight," she said. "I should go. Before it's too late."

"It's already too late, Natalie."

There was no mistaking the meaning of his words, the implicit promise behind them. She shook her head, almost desperately. "I really have to go."

He stepped back. "Then go."

She did, accepting the reprieve even though she knew he'd let her run, but he wouldn't let her hide.

Natalie had just stepped out of the shower the next morning when there was a knock at the door. She frowned, squinting at the face of her watch on the countertop. It wasn't even seven-thirty. She rubbed the towel briskly over her body as the knock sounded again, more impatiently this time.

"Hold on a minute," she grumbled, slipping her arms into her robe.

She hung her towel back over the rack and padded across the thick carpet toward the door. She could only think of one person who would have the audacity to show up at her door at such an hour, and if it *was* him—he'd better have coffee.

She peeked through the peephole, not at all surprised to find Lieutenant Creighton standing in the hall, not at all surprised by the way her heart jumped around in her chest. She wasn't ready to face him. Not yet. Not after last night—the way he'd kissed her; the way she'd kissed him back. But she wasn't going to hide, either.

She unfastened the safety chain and opened the door. "What are you doing here?"

"I brought you breakfast."

He smiled, and the flash of dimples caused some of her irritation to dissipate. But she wouldn't let him know he could get around her with a smile.

She scowled. "I don't eat breakfast."

"I promised you cereal." He held up the grocery bag he carried in one hand. The other hand was behind his back. "I brought cereal. And milk."

"I'm lactose intolerant," she grumbled.

"I doubt that—since I saw you dump about half a gallon of cream in your coffee at the courthouse the other day."

"That's because the courthouse coffee is intolerable without it."

"Maybe this will be more to your liking." He brought his other hand from behind his back, and Natalie nearly wept with gratitude when she recognized the green paper cup from the hotel's gourmet café.

He grinned. "You want it?"

"Please." She wasn't averse to begging.

"Then you have to invite me in to share breakfast."

"You can have the whole box of cereal," she promised. "As long as I get the coffee."

He handed her the cup. "Not just coffee," he said, stepping into the room. "But a vanilla latte with cinnamon."

She reverently lifted the lid from the cup and inhaled deeply. "How did you know?"

"I didn't," he admitted. "It was noted on the board as today's featured flavor."

"It's an addiction." She dipped a fingertip into the foam, licked it off. "I'd be your slave for life—if only you'd brought biscotti."

She didn't realize how suggestive were her actions and her

words until he cleared his throat and moved around her. "I'll keep that in mind."

Maybe she should have been embarrassed, but after the sleepless night she'd spent thinking about him, it was gratifying to know that he wasn't unaffected.

She took her coffee and sat at the tiny table in the kitchenette while the lieutenant rummaged through the cupboard for a bowl. She liked to watch him. His movements were confident yet somehow graceful, his hands were wide palmed with long fingers. Strong hands, skilled hands. She remembered, vividly, how those hands had skimmed over her body, how his fingers had teased her aching breasts.

She forced her gaze away, focused it on her coffee, tried to ignore the heat she felt in her cheeks. She lifted the cup to her lips and swallowed a mouthful of coffee. Very hot coffee. She gasped, coughed.

Creighton glanced up, carton of milk in hand. "Are you okay?"

Other than feeling like a complete imbecile... "Fine."

He brought his bowl over to the table, sat down across from her. "Snap, Krackle and Pop" filled the silence. The lieutenant's choice of cereal was also Jack's favorite, and the familiar sound brought a sharp pang of longing.

He dug into his breakfast; she sipped her latte, carefully.

When he'd emptied the bowl, he pushed it aside and pinned her with his gaze. She folded both hands around her cup and braced herself.

"I'm not going to forget what happened last night just because you want me to."

"It won't happen again," she assured him.

His lips curved in a slow smile. "Now that sounds an awful lot like a challenge."

She shook her head. "It's not. I'm not being coy or playing hard to get. I'm just telling you how it is."

"Then you're deluding yourself."

She didn't think his statement warranted any kind of response.

"Whether you like it or not, whether you want to admit it or not, there's something happening between us."

"Nothing's going to happen that I don't want to happen."

"You wanted me last night, Natalie." The soft words floated on the air as seductively as a kiss.

He was right, and she'd lain awake long after she'd turned out the lights, unable to forget the feel of his hands on her body, the pressure of his lips against her own, the aching emptiness in her heart.

"You wanted me as much as I wanted you," he continued. "And then you got scared."

She forced a laugh. "Scared?"

He nodded.

"Of what?"

"Losing control."

She sipped her coffee, refused to give him the satisfaction of disagreeing. But he was wrong. She wasn't afraid—there was nothing to be afraid of, because she simply wasn't going to lose control. She wasn't going to make that mistake again.

"Not even a token denial?" he taunted.

"You brought me coffee, Lieutenant, which inclines me favorably toward you. But you're not so irresistible that I'm going to throw all common sense aside and jump your bones."

"What if I'd brought biscotti?"

She allowed herself a small smile. "Maybe."

Chapter 6

Dylan liked to see her smile. It was something, in his opinion, she did far too seldom. He wondered again what had happened in her thirty-one years to dim the spark he'd only caught brief glimpses of in her eyes.

She'd been in town about a month, he'd known her less than half of that time. He certainly didn't know her well. But he did know that Natalie Vaughn had barriers all around her, and while she seemed perfectly content living behind those barriers, she'd been terrified at the possibility he might break through them.

What made her so wary? Was she uncomfortable with men in general? Or was it his status as a cop that unnerved her?

Despite her casual rebuttal, her confident assurance that he wasn't irresistible, he'd seen the uneasiness in her eyes. Just as he'd seen the flare of awareness when he'd first mentioned the kiss. The damn kiss that had kept him awake all night.

He hadn't intended for things to go as far as they had. He hadn't intended to kiss her at all. He'd thought about it, a lot, over the past several days. And he'd thought of at least a dozen reasons why pursuing the attraction he felt was a bad idea. But in that moment, he hadn't been able to think of a single one.

Maybe he'd been testing her, maybe testing himself. He wanted to see if there was any foundation to the chemistry he felt whenever they were in the same room together.

In the first instant that his lips touched hers, he'd expected resistance. He'd counted on it. And when he'd found nothing but softly yielding acceptance, he'd been lost.

She'd been soft and warm and so incredibly responsive, and he'd wanted nothing more than to lift her into his arms and carry her down the hall to his bedroom. He'd wanted to lay her down on top of the comforter and slowly strip off her clothes, to lay down beside her and spend the rest of the night making love—

He severed the thought abruptly, more shaken by his own thoughts than he wanted to admit. He was past the point of denying how much he wanted her, but he'd accepted the attraction as a purely physical urge. He'd had sex with other women, but he'd never made love with anyone but Beth. He'd never wanted to. But he couldn't deny there was something about Natalie that drew him. Something stronger than the desire he'd felt for anyone else in the past four years.

And he wanted another taste of her. He wanted to know if his memory of the kiss they'd shared had been enhanced by the erotic dreams he'd had the previous evening. Dreams in which Natalie had played a starring role.

After the way she'd retreated the previous evening, he'd decided it would be best to give her some space. But she'd been his first thought when he awoke, and he'd had a moment to savor the pleasure, the possibility, before guilt had intruded. He should be thinking of Beth, not Natalie. But with every day that passed, it required more of an effort to conjure Beth's sweet smile and laughing brown eyes. Maybe it was a sign that he was finally beginning to heal, but he still felt a pang of loss and longing for the woman he'd loved. And a sharper, stronger tug of need for the woman in front of him now.

"Thanks for the coffee," Natalie said, interrupting his thoughts. "But I need to kick you out now so I can get ready for work."

He took his bowl and spoon to the small sink and rinsed them under the tap. "Why are you so determined to keep me at a distance?"

To her credit, she considered his question before responding. "I keep everyone at a distance."

"Why?"

"It's easier that way."

"And lonelier." He would know. He'd done the same thing for a long time—until she came to town.

"I have no complaints," she assured him.

He stepped toward her, pleased that she stood her ground even though she had to tilt her head to meet his gaze. "None?"

She swallowed, but her eyes—wide, wary, and aware—remained level with his. "No."

He didn't believe her. He wasn't even sure she believed it herself. "Why are you fighting what's happening between us?"

She lifted her chin defiantly. "I don't owe you any explanations just because I won't fall into bed with you."

"No, you don't," he agreed. "But you do need to understand that it will happen."

"Excuse me?"

He grinned at her indignant response. "I'd prefer sooner rather than later, but I can wait."

"I am *not* going to get involved with you."

"We're already involved."

"A few kisses don't equal a relationship."

He didn't argue with her. He knew her well enough to know that pushing would only push her away. Instead, he cupped her face in his hands. The defiant glint in her eyes faded away.

"We all have our ghosts, Natalie. But if we don't learn to live with them, we're not really living."

It was something he'd heard so many times since Beth had died, something he was only beginning to understand himself. Then he very gently, and very briefly, touched his lips to hers. "Have a good day."

She waited until she heard the door click shut behind him, then let out a long, shaky breath.

She'd thought her experience with Eric had immunized her against men. One kiss from Dylan Creighton had proven otherwise. One kiss had banished all the painful memories from her mind, leaving only a desperate, almost painful, yearning. She wanted Dylan, she couldn't deny that. She also couldn't let herself succumb to the desire.

She'd been so hurt when Eric walked out, devastated that he'd turned his back, not just on her but on their child, and she'd vowed that no one would ever have the power to hurt her again. If she opened up to Dylan, invariably, she would start to hope, to dream, and she'd get hurt.

We all have our ghosts, Natalie. But if we don't learn to live with them, we're not really living.

His words stayed with Natalie throughout the day, and for a long time afterward. She tried to dismiss his statement as self-serving, which it undoubtedly was. "A man will say anything to get you into bed," Shannon had often warned. Natalie had refused to believe it. She'd learned the hard way that her sister was right. Seven years later, she knew she wouldn't ever make that mistake again.

But she couldn't deny that there was some legitimacy to Dylan's statement. If she continued to live her life in fear of repeating the mistakes of her past, she wasn't really in control of her life. By refusing to open herself up to intimacy, she was letting Jack's father control her future.

She sighed and tucked a strand of hair behind her ear. Did it really make sense? Or was she merely looking for an excuse to succumb to the attraction she felt for Dylan?

And when had she started thinking of him as "Dylan" anyway?

He was Lieutenant Creighton, a professional acquaintance, a colleague, and it was best if she continued to think of him as such.

But sometime over the past week, some of the barriers had dropped. Or maybe the last of her resistance had melted away with the brief touch of his lips to hers.

She shook her head. It was a good thing she was going back to Chicago this weekend. She needed to spend time with Jack, to remember her priorities. She had neither the time nor the inclination for a personal involvement, no matter how much her hormones might wish otherwise.

She flipped through the calendar on her desk, as if she needed to count the days. As if she didn't know there were exactly fifteen more days until school was out. Fifteen more days without her son. She'd see him on weekends, of course, but two days out of every seven wasn't enough.

She was so tempted to pack it in and go home. To run away from Fairweather, back to Chicago and everything that was familiar.

She sighed. Except that her reasons for leaving were still

valid. She wanted something better for Jack than what they had in Chicago. A better home, a better school, better opportunities.

Her pay increase as an assistant district attorney wasn't significant, but the cost of living was considerably less in Fairweather. Besides, she'd been given a nest egg—and a fairly substantial one at that. Which was the most important reason she'd had for taking this job: she'd made a promise.

But at what cost? It was a question she'd pondered ever since the opportunity had presented itself. What would the ultimate cost of her decision be? And would Jack ever forgive her for what she'd done?

She was tempted, more than she wanted to admit, to forget the bargain had ever been made. But leaving Fairweather now, just because she was feeling unsettled and insecure, before she'd even made an effort, would be cowardly. She was anything but a coward.

I can't figure out if you're incredibly brave or incredibly stupid.

Dylan's words echoed in the back of her mind. Well, that makes two of us, she thought.

And yet, the man who'd raked her over the coals at Roger Merrick's apartment was the same man who'd bantered with her over breakfast, comforted her during the storm, kissed her mindless the night before.

She almost wished he'd stayed angry with her. Anger she could handle. She had no defense against the unfamiliar emotions that he'd stirred inside her with a simple look, a touch, a kiss. Wants, needs, too long denied, had reawakened.

Yeah, she was tempted to run, but she wasn't going to. Not this time. She was determined to make a home for Jack and herself, to put down roots so her son would feel that he belonged. That was her ultimate goal, and she wouldn't let anyone or anything dissuade her.

* * *

Natalie was busy in court throughout most of the following week, and she guessed that Lieutenant Creighton must have been occupied with his own work because she didn't see him at all over the next several days. But every morning when she stopped at the hotel café for her latte, she thought of him.

It was silly, she knew, to make a big deal out of something that clearly wasn't, but she couldn't stop speculating about the man who'd been thoughtful enough to bring her coffee. Obviously there was more to the lieutenant than she'd originally believed.

Just as obviously, his absence since that early-morning visit affirmed her earlier supposition: he'd lost interest. He'd made a pass, she'd deflected it—okay, she'd succumbed and then deflected, but the end result was the same: he'd moved on. She wasn't surprised; she was relieved. And maybe, although she'd never admit it, just a little bit disappointed.

She didn't have time to dwell on his absence. She had too much work to do to allow herself to be distracted by anything or anyone. Until he showed up at her office again Friday afternoon.

"You haven't been around here very much this week," Creighton said. "Have you been busy or just avoiding me?"

She ignored the quick surge of pleasure at his appearance, and her voice, when she spoke, was carefully neutral. "I've been busy," she assured him. "I've spent most of my waking hours in court this week."

And most of her sleeping hours dreaming about the lieutenant's mind-numbing kisses, but she kept that detail to herself.

"You've done quite well, from what I've heard."

She had to take a mental step back. She was the only one who'd been thinking—obsessing—about his kiss. *He* was talking about court. To hide her embarrassment, she busied herself sorting through the stack of files on her desk. "Checking up on me, Lieutenant?"

"I told you before—it's a small town."

"Apparently so."

"You went four for five this week."

"Three were pleas," she told him.

"Defendants only plead when they know they can't win."

She shrugged. "I'm only working with the evidence I've been given. It's your detectives who deserve the credit more than I."

"Very diplomatic, Natalie. But I've seen prosecutors blow cases with apparently overwhelming evidence."

"And I've seen cases lost because of improper investigative techniques."

"Touché."

She stuffed a pile of folders into her briefcase. How was she supposed to carry on a casual conversation when all she could think about was getting him naked? "Was there a particular reason you stopped by, Lieutenant?"

He ignored her question, leaned a hip against the corner of her desk. "Don't you think we've moved beyond the formalities of titles?"

The fragrance of his aftershave was subtle; the effect of his proximity on her hormones not even close to subtle. She shifted a little farther away from him, cleared her throat.

"No," she responded belatedly to his question. Her use of his rank was deliberate, a reminder to both of them of their working relationship. She couldn't allow herself to think of him as anything other than a colleague. She didn't dare think of him as a man.

"Were you thinking of me as a cop when you kissed me?"

She thought he would have forgotten about that kiss. She wished she could. "Obviously, I wasn't thinking at all."

"Why is that obvious?"

"Because if I'd been thinking, it wouldn't have happened." She concentrated on rearranging the files in her briefcase.

She was surprised, and relieved, when he didn't pursue the topic any further. Instead, he said, "I thought maybe I'd take you out to dinner—to celebrate your success this week."

"Thanks, but, um, I can't."

"You already have plans for dinner?"

"Yes." And she was grateful she did. Dinner, she instinctively knew, would only be a prelude to something more, and she wasn't ready for that next step.

"Maybe tomorrow then?"

"Actually, I'm going back to Chicago for the weekend," she admitted.

"Oh."

Natalie sifted through the pink slips on her desk.

"I met with Ellis Todd yesterday," he said.

She continued to rifle through her messages. "The accountant?"

He nodded. "Apparently my original information wasn't up-to-date. Mr. Todd left the accounting firm of Denby & Witter almost three years ago. He now works for Zane Conroy."

That got her attention. She dropped the pink slips. "I guess you were right," she murmured. "It all comes back to Conroy."

"Yeah," he agreed, but he didn't sound very pleased about it.

"What's the problem?"

"I'm not sure. I know I should be thrilled by this information, it's just that—" he shook his head. "I interviewed this guy, and I can't see him pulling the trigger. I've never met anyone who seems less likely to take another man's life."

"The one thing I've learned in my experience in criminal law is to expect the unexpected," she told him.

He nodded. "I know. But he seemed genuinely surprised—

shocked even—to learn that his gun had been used in a murder." He scrubbed a hand through his hair. "Then again, Conroy doesn't hire idiots."

"How did he explain the gun?"

"He said he'd bought it for his wife."

"Why?"

"Because they were separated, and he was worried about her being on her own."

Natalie frowned. "Did he have any reason to think his wife was in danger?"

"He didn't say. Although he definitely seemed to be holding something back. And when I spoke to the wife—who, it turns out, is Zane Conroy's cousin—I got the same impression."

"What did she say about the gun?"

"That she always keeps it in the safe in her closet. But when she went to get it—"

"It was gone," Natalie guessed.

"Yeah."

"What's your take on the wife?"

"Young, pretty—in a fragile sort of way."

She resisted—barely—the urge to roll her eyes. It figured that was the kind of woman who would appeal to him: someone who needed to be taken care of, protected. She pushed aside the thought. "Do you think she's capable of murder?"

"I think *anyone* is capable of murder, given the right circumstances."

She didn't quite bite back her sigh of exasperation. "Do you think she killed Merrick?"

"No," he admitted. "And she has an alibi for the night of the murder."

"Does the husband?"

"Yet another fact that doesn't quite fit," he told her. "He

says he was at the office, claimed video surveillance tapes of the building would show he didn't leave until after midnight."

"Did you get the tapes?"

"We're working on it. Conroy owns the building, and he refused to give us anything without a warrant."

"Even evidence that might exculpate an employee?"

Creighton shrugged. "I didn't expect cooperation from Conroy. And the tapes should be in my hands tomorrow in any event."

She nodded, glanced at her watch. As much as she wanted to be kept apprised of the details in the investigation, right now she wanted to be on her way to Chicago even more.

"I guess I'm holding you up," he said.

"I'm sorry." She forced the lid of her briefcase down, struggled to close the locks. "But I really do have to be going. I appreciate you stopping by, though, to keep me up-to-date."

Creighton nodded again. "No problem. Enjoy your weekend."

She smiled, her thoughts and her heart already in Chicago. "I will."

Throughout the weekend, Dylan continued to review the evidence piling up in the Merrick investigation. But whenever he had a free moment—and often when he should have been concentrating on something else—his thoughts strayed to Natalie.

He wondered where she was, who she was with, what she was doing. She obviously had ties in Illinois, but she'd taken a job in Pennsylvania. Why? Was it really as simple as she claimed? He knew he should accept her explanation. There was no reason for him to continue speculating about her reasons for coming to Fairweather, but he couldn't shake the feeling that she was hiding something.

We all have our ghosts, he'd told her. And it was true. How could he judge Natalie for not opening up to him when he continued to hide his own secrets?

Every day he lived with the knowledge of what had happened to Beth. He didn't talk about it; he tried not to think about it. But every day he suffered with the truth of what he'd never been able to tell anyone: he'd killed her.

He hadn't fired the bullets that had taken her life, but he was responsible for her death. He was the reason she'd been in that alley. Died in that alley.

Yet he found himself thinking more about Natalie than Beth these days. While there was a part of him that couldn't help feeling guilty about this fact, another part reveled in the realization. He'd been haunted by the events of that one night for four years now, living each day in an attempt to make amends for the past.

Since Natalie had come into his life, he'd started looking forward. For the first time in a long time, he cared about the future. Maybe he really was ready to move on. If only he could convince her to move on with him.

So predominant was she in his thoughts that Dylan wasn't at all surprised when he answered his cell phone Monday night and heard Natalie's voice. What surprised and worried him was the obvious strain in her voice.

"Lieutenant Creighton?"

"What is it, Natalie?"

"I need you to come to the hotel. Please."

He didn't ask any more questions until he got there.

She opened the door immediately. Her eyes were shadowed, her cheeks pale, but she offered him a wan smile. "Sorry to bother you after hours," she said, "but I didn't really know who else to call."

He put his hands on her shoulders gently, felt some of her tension ease. "What's going on?"

She crossed the room to the desk, handed him a large unmarked envelope. Despite her obvious agitation, her hand was steady. "This was on the desk when I got in."

He opened the flap of the envelope and pulled out the photographs. There were four 8x10s in glossy, gruesome full color, depicting the murder of Roger Merrick. The first was apparently taken after the first shot was fired: the front of his shirt showed a single bullet hole, blood already soaking the fabric. His eyes were wide, unfocused, empty. There was no doubt in Dylan's mind that he was already dead.

The second picture showed a wider hole in his chest, the glint of white bone through the destruction of tissue and muscle. Photos three and four were more of the same, showing more damage to the body after each successive bullet had ripped into it, until there was little more than a bloody, pulpy mess left.

He shoved the pictures back into the envelope. Natalie was standing with her back against the wall, her arms folded over her chest, her eyes focused on the opposite wall. He could only imagine how she must have felt to come into the sanctity of her room and find the envelope. Then to open the envelope and face the images caught in those photos.

"I want you to check out of the hotel."

She finally turned to face him. "Haven't we been through this already?"

"Someone was here—in your room. Are you having difficulty grasping that fact?"

"Of course not," she denied hotly. "But it's equally obvious that someone is trying to intimidate me, and I won't be intimidated."

He shook his head, but what he really wanted to do was shake *her*. Dammit, why couldn't she see that she was in danger? Why wouldn't she listen to him? Why hadn't Beth listened to him?

He forced aside the haunting memories. "Please, Natalie. You need to take this seriously."

"I am taking it seriously. I'm just not running away."

He gave up, only because he knew she was too stubborn to listen to reason. And because he planned to call Joel Logan. Joel's partner at Courtland & Logan Investigations was Michael Courtland, whose family owned the Courtland Hotel chain. Before Dylan left the hotel tonight, he'd make sure there was security outside Natalie's room.

He pulled his cell phone out of his pocket and called for a couple of uniforms. He wanted the envelope and the photos taken to the crime lab, and he wanted the hotel staff thoroughly interrogated. When the officers arrived, he left Natalie's room only long enough to give them instructions and to grab a local newspaper.

By the time he returned to her room, she was seated behind the desk, back at work. He could almost admire the ease with which she put the pictures out of her mind, if he didn't worry that she was too easily disregarding the potential danger to herself. He tossed the newspaper onto the desk.

"What's this?"

"The classified section of today's paper."

"Why?"

"Because you need to find somewhere else to stay."

She picked up the paper, set it aside on top of the pile of files stacked on the floor beside the desk.

"Aren't you even going to look at it?"

"I've already found a place."

"Oh." He lowered himself onto the edge of the bed, facing her desk. "Why didn't you mention that when I asked you to check out of the hotel?"

"Because you didn't ask, you ordered. I won't be manipulated by whoever put those photos in my room, and I won't be manipulated by you."

"I wasn't trying to manipulate you," he denied.

"Weren't you?"

He let her comment drop. "Where are you moving to?" he asked instead.

"The west end, on Oakridge."

It was one of the more upscale parts of town and he hadn't realized there were any apartments there, but he couldn't fault her choice. "Nice area."

"I'm glad you approve," she said dryly.

"Okay. It's none of my business. Point taken." He hesitated a second, then, "When do you move in?"

She smiled, shaking her head. "The twentieth."

"Good." He stood, prepared to leave so that she could get back to work.

"Lieutenant."

The softly spoken word halted him in his tracks. He turned around. "Yes?"

"Why are you so determined to protect me?"

There was no point in trying to deny it. Nor was there any point in trying to explain it. No one could understand the devastating loss he'd suffered, the sense of emptiness that still haunted him, the guilt that never lessened. So all he said was, "I like you, Natalie, and I don't want to see you get hurt."

"I take care of myself," she reminded him, then softened the words with a smile. "But thanks."

He nodded and forced himself to walk out the door before he did something really crazy—like haul her into his arms and hold on to her forever. Because he knew that nothing was forever.

Chapter 7

The arrest of Ellis Todd for the murder of Roger Merrick was the top news story the following morning. With the touch of a button, Natalie turned off the radio and silenced the reports. If only she could shut off her mind so easily.

The photos of Merrick's murder had shaken her more than she wanted to admit. Not just the image of his ravaged body, which was indelibly imprinted on her mind already, but the fact that someone had taken pictures during his execution. What kind of a person would do something like that? And why would they send the pictures to her?

She managed to push these questions from her mind while she reviewed the file for an upcoming shoplifting trial. She was happy dealing with petty thefts and vandalism. She'd be even happier if she never heard of Roger Merrick or Ellis Todd again.

John Beckett effectively trampled her happiness by dropping a new file on her desk later that morning.

"The prelim's scheduled for next Monday."

She glanced at the label on the file, and her stomach tightened. She was new at this job; she didn't have the right to pick and choose her cases. "This is going to be a high-profile case. Why are you giving it to me?"

"You don't think you're up to it?"

It was a deliberate challenge, and she knew it. She didn't know why. "I just thought you'd want to handle every step of this proceeding yourself."

"Ordinarily I would," he agreed. "I have a conflict on the date that's been set for the prelim."

The date that *he* set for the prelim.

"I know I could have asked for another date," he continued, anticipating her argument. "But Hawkins was adamant that this matter move forward as quickly as possible."

"Hawkins?"

Beckett frowned. "Didn't you see the news this morning? Randolph Hawkins is representing Ellis Todd on this charge."

Could her day possibly get any worse?

"What if he wants to call me as a witness? After all, I did find the body." It was a subtle hint to her boss of the potential conflict of interest, an unspoken request that he reassign the case.

"He assured me that's not a possibility. You didn't see anything in that room that pertains to the murder itself."

No, just what was left of the victim.

Beckett glanced at his watch. "I've got to run. I'm meeting the mayor for lunch. If you have any other questions, we can deal with them later."

With those last words, he walked out, leaving Natalie alone with a lot of unanswered questions and an unwanted assignment until Dylan walked into her office a short while later.

"I wanted to let you know that we arrested Ellis Todd for the murder of Roger Merrick."

"It was on the radio this morning. Apparently you changed your mind about accountants as criminals."

"It's hard to dispute the evidence," he told her.

"What kind of evidence?"

"The gun was registered in his name, his prints were on the clip, and he doesn't have any alibi for the time of the murder."

"The surveillance tapes didn't confirm his story?"

Dylan shook his head. "They showed him leaving the building at 6:40 p.m. the night of the murder and not returning until 8:15 the following morning."

She frowned. "Why would he tell you he was there if he knew the tapes would show he wasn't?"

"Maybe he didn't know the entrance was under surveillance. Maybe he forgot about the surveillance. Who knows why people say the things they do?"

"It seems like a careless mistake."

"Like filing down the serial number."

"Hmm." She seemed to consider that for a minute. "What about motive?"

"As I said, anyone is capable of anything, given the right circumstances."

"What do you think drove Conroy's accountant to kill Roger Merrick?"

"I haven't figured that out yet," he admitted. "Maybe it was as simple as 'kill or be killed.'"

"What about the pictures?"

He lowered himself into an empty chair across from her desk. "Yeah, there are some things that don't fit together neatly. I can't see Todd pausing between bullets to take photos of his victim. Maybe he's a psychopath, maybe there was someone else with him. But right now, he's the one we've got."

"And now I've got him," she grumbled.

"What do you mean?"

"John Beckett assigned the case to me."

"You've got to be kidding."

His disbelief was obvious, and put her back up. "You don't think I can handle it?"

"You shouldn't have to," he protested. "You found his body."

"Gee, I'd almost forgotten that," she said dryly.

He didn't crack a smile. "What the hell was Beckett thinking—putting you in the position of having to prosecute the murderer?"

"Maybe he was thinking that I'm capable of doing the job."

"I don't doubt that," he said. "But every step of the proceeding will bring back memories of that night."

She nodded. Not that she'd forgotten, but she still wasn't looking forward to reviewing the crime-scene photos and autopsy report in their graphic, gruesome detail.

Dylan shook his head. "It just doesn't make any sense. This case is guaranteed to garner headlines. Why would Beckett give it up?"

It was the same question she'd wondered about, and she'd come to one conclusion. "Maybe he doesn't think we can win it," she said. "And if we lose, it won't be his loss. On the other hand, if we get a conviction, he can take the credit for assigning the case to me."

He finally managed a smile. "That's just the sort of thing Beckett would do," he agreed. "Although I didn't expect you would have figured him out so quickly."

She shrugged. "Putting me in the hot seat covers his own butt. It's a smart move politically—if not one I'm thrilled with personally."

"I can give you any help you need," he offered.

"I will want to go over the evidence with you in detail, once I've had a chance to review the file more carefully," she told him.

"No problem."

"But I do have one question now."

"What's that?"

She met his gaze evenly. "Why is your signature on every report and every witness statement in the file?"

Dylan hadn't thought she would pick up on that. Not that it mattered, really, he just hadn't expected she'd notice such a detail on a cursory review of the evidence.

"It's my case," he said simply.

"You're a lieutenant. Aren't you in the habit of delegating?"

"Not where Conroy is concerned."

She twirled her pen in her fingers. "What is the reason for your obsession with Conroy?"

"He's scum and I want him off the streets."

"You must want him badly to have put in so much overtime on this case."

"Are you worried about the department's budget?"

"Not at all," she denied. "I just want to know if you have a personal stake in making this case that may backfire against us at trial."

"My personal stakes are just that," he said coolly.

She tucked a stray lock of hair behind her ear and sighed. "We're on the same side here, Lieutenant. If there's something you're not telling me, it could jeopardize the effectiveness of the prosecution."

"Everything you need to know is in the file."

"Is it?"

While Dylan inwardly cursed her perception, he was impressed by her instincts. She might be young and new to the job, but she was handling it. And she wasn't cutting him any slack.

"I'm not going to claim that I'm completely impartial with respect to Conroy, but I did a thorough and careful job on this investigation."

She remained seated but tilted her head to meet his gaze. "If you want me to do my job, you have to give me all the facts."

"The facts are in the file."

"Tell me what's not in the file."

He didn't want to talk about it. He didn't want to *think* about it. But Natalie was right. She needed to know.

"It happened four years ago," he said.

She sat quietly, patiently, waiting.

It would be easier if she didn't look at him. He didn't want to see the pity in her eyes.

"On the south side of town—just a few blocks over from Roger Merrick's apartment building." Years later, he could still picture the scene as if it were yesterday. He still suffered whenever the image came to mind.

"There was a young reporter," he continued, "recently transferred from the current-events department of the local newspaper to the crime section. She got information, indirectly and illegally, about a major bust that was about to go down."

He stared at the framed certificates behind her desk. It wasn't so hard if he pretended it was someone else's case, someone else's life.

"Determined to headline the next day's papers, she took her notepad and camera to the location of the scheduled take-down." He didn't dare blink. If he closed his eyes for even half a second he'd see her body lying there, unmoving, as her life drained away into a crimson puddle on the sidewalk. He'd heard the sirens in the distance—too far away. Too late to save her.

"She made the headlines all right," he said bitterly. "Reporter Slain In Botched Drug Bust."

It had been front-page news for too long. And not long enough. Within a few weeks, her name had disappeared from the papers. With no evidence and no leads, there was nothing to report. Eventually people forgot. Except Dylan. He'd never forgotten; he never would forget.

He finally looked at Natalie. Her eyes were filled with compassion and understanding—as if anyone could possibly understand.

He took a deep breath. "Her name was Beth. She was my wife."

She'd asked him to tell her. She'd practically demanded an explanation. But Natalie hadn't expected this.

Dylan had told her he wasn't married. She'd mistakenly assumed he never had been. Now that she knew the circumstances behind his wife's death, she understood why he hadn't mentioned it. Four years later, he was still suffering the loss, and she regretted that she'd had to force the issue.

"I'm sorry." The words were hopelessly inadequate, but she didn't know what else to say.

"Conroy was behind it," he continued. "Just because I couldn't prove it doesn't mean it isn't true."

"And you've been after Conroy ever since," she guessed.

He didn't deny it, didn't apologize for it. "She was twenty-nine years old. Too young to die. Too innocent to die like that."

She understood his need to find justice for the woman he'd loved, and she hoped he would. But she knew only too well how that single-minded purpose might ultimately undermine their case. If Hawkins knew about Dylan's wife—and it seemed that everyone knew everything about everyone else in this town—he'd claim bias against his client, which could taint any of the evidence Dylan had found. In this case—everything.

But there was no point in bringing that up now. At least now that she was aware of it, she could prepare for it. "Did you know Hawkins is representing Todd?"

He nodded. "Todd started asking for him as soon as we brought him in."

"Doesn't that strike you as odd? That Hawkins would defend the man accused of killing Merrick?"

"Conroy keeps him on retainer. Hawkins goes wherever Conroy sends him."

"Still, I would think that representing the man who murdered a former client would be, if not unethical, at least immoral?"

"Hawkins doesn't concern himself with morals or ethics."

She frowned. There was so much she still didn't know about the players in this drama, and she knew that could be a disadvantage in court. But for tonight, she'd uncovered enough.

It had obviously been difficult for Dylan to talk about his wife's murder, but she was glad he'd told her. He was a man who'd suffered a devastating loss, yet he'd endured. Which made her feel like a coward for clinging so steadfastly to a pain that couldn't compare to his own.

Maybe it was time to let go of those ghosts. Or at least learn to live with them. "Are you hungry?"

"What?" He looked at her blankly.

"Are you hungry?" she asked again. "Because I'm starving. And I thought maybe, if you didn't have any plans for dinner, you might want to grab a bite with me."

He managed a smile. "No plans."

"I know a great place that does veggie burgers with alfalfa sprouts and—"

"How about chili?" he countered.

"Chili sounds great."

Dylan didn't know why she'd invited him to share dinner with her, but he was glad. Talking about Beth, replaying the events of that horrific night, had been difficult. He didn't think he'd ever remember his wife without feeling guilt and regret. But what he'd realized, as he'd told Natalie about the circumstances of her death, was that it was starting to hurt a little less. He was beginning to heal.

And he knew that Natalie was a part of that process. Before she'd come into his life, he hadn't wanted anything more than his simple, solitary existence. He did now.

"Who makes the best chili in town?" She was standing beside her car, waiting for his directions.

"It's a small place downtown with limited parking. Why don't you come with me, and I'll bring you back here later to pick up your car?"

She shrugged. "All right. If you're sure you don't mind."

"It's no problem," he assured her. And this way, when she figured out where he was taking her, she couldn't back out.

She figured it out quickly. "This is a very residential area. And vaguely familiar."

"My house is just around the corner."

"I thought we were going for chili."

"We are."

She looked skeptical, but made no further protest.

He parked his car and led her through the side door, directly into the kitchen. She stopped, inhaled deeply. "Oh. Wow. It smells wonderful."

"I put everything in the slow cooker this morning. It tastes better if it has several hours for the flavors to mingle."

She went over to the pot, lifted the lid to examine the contents. "You really made this?"

"I did."

He took a spoon from the drawer, offered her a sample. "Careful, it's hot."

She blew gently, then opened her mouth for a taste.

"Mmm." She swallowed. "I hate to admit it, but this is the best chili I've ever had. You really do know your way around a kitchen, don't you?"

"What did you think—my invitation to make you dinner was a ploy to get you to my bedroom?"

She shifted guiltily. "Maybe."

He grinned. "And maybe it was, but I would have cooked for you first."

She laughed. "I'll set the table."

He sliced a loaf of crusty bread and poured red wine into two glasses. "The bottle was open," he explained. "It's the secret ingredient in my chili."

"Not anymore."

He shrugged. "But you don't know what else is in here," he told her, scooping generous amounts of chili into two bowls.

She carried the bowls to the table and they ate in companionable silence. She was only halfway through hers before she pushed it away in defeat.

"I'd almost forgotten what a home-cooked meal tastes like," she told him. "That was delicious. Thank you."

"Anytime."

She smiled. "I'd better warn you—now that I've tasted your cooking, I might take you up on that offer."

He refilled her glass. "I wouldn't have made the offer if I hadn't meant it."

"You're a very nice man, Lieutenant."

"No, I'm just trying to get you into my bed."

She picked up her wine, sipped. "I don't know whether or not you're joking."

"I'm not."

"It's not going to happen."

"Not tonight," he agreed. "If you slept with me tonight, I'd wonder if it was just because you felt sorry for me."

She smiled. "Does that happen often—women having sex with you because they feel sorry for you?"

"Not to my knowledge," he said dryly. "But I did wonder if that was why you offered to have dinner with me."

She shook her head. "No."

It was the simplicity of her response that convinced him it was true.

"I didn't want to tell you about Beth," he admitted. "Because I didn't want you to look at me with pity.

"It was horrible after she died—not just dealing with the fact that she wasn't around anymore, but the way everyone tiptoed around me as if I might suddenly fall apart." He thought back, smiled wryly. "For a time, maybe it was true. But I got past that. I wish everyone else would."

Natalie pushed away from the table, carried their bowls to the sink. "I don't feel sorry for you." She turned back to face him. "I feel sad for you, for everything you've been through. And I admire you, for having survived."

He didn't deserve her admiration, but he wasn't inclined to disillusion her. He liked that she could look at him and see someone worthy. It made him want to be worthy.

He stood up, moved toward her. "I'm glad you're here, Natalie."

She swallowed. "Me, too."

He wanted to kiss her. In that moment, he wanted nothing more. He'd sampled the softness of her lips, tasted her intoxicating flavor, enjoyed a hint of the passion he knew burned inside her.

If he kissed her now, she'd kiss him back. Maybe that kiss would lead to something more. But he knew that if he pushed her too far, too fast, he'd scare her away, and that was a risk he wasn't willing to take.

"Come on," he said. "I'll drive you back to your car."

* * *

Friday night came and for the first time since she'd taken the A.D.A. position in Fairweather, Natalie wasn't on a plane to Chicago. The Ellis Todd prelim was scheduled to begin on Monday and she had to focus her time and attention on that. The knowledge didn't stop her from missing Jack.

She reminded herself again that she'd taken this job for her son. Everything she'd done in the past seven years, every decision she'd made, had been for Jack. The reminder didn't make the emptiness inside any more bearable.

She still believed that this move to Fairweather would ultimately be best for him. For both of them. But the separation was almost more than she could handle. She would give anything to hold him right now, to feel the slight weight of his slender arms wrapped tight around her, to breathe in the unique scent of her child. She closed her eyes, pictured his smiling face, the handful of freckles sprinkled over the bridge of his nose. She blinked away the tears that sprang to her eyes. If she gave in now, she wouldn't be able to stop crying.

She might not be able to wrap her arms around him long distance, but she could at least hear his voice. She picked up the phone and dialed her sister's number. Shannon answered on the second ring.

"Can I talk to Jack?" she asked, after she'd chatted with her sister a few minutes.

"Actually, he isn't here right now," Shannon told her.

Natalie's heart sank a little further. "What do you mean? Where is he?"

"Connor's dad had tickets to the White Sox game tonight, and he asked if Jack wanted to go along."

"Oh." She knew her son would have been thrilled with the invitation, but understanding his excitement failed to lessen her disappointment.

"He's been miserable all week because he knew you weren't coming home this weekend. I thought the ball game might take his mind off of missing you for a few hours."

Although she was sure it wasn't intended, she felt the censure in her sister's words. As if it was Natalie's fault that Jack was unhappy. "I've been miserable without him, too," she pointed out.

"I know," Shannon said gently. "I can have him call you when he gets home."

"No," she said. "He'll be more than ready for bed by then. Just give him a big hug and a kiss from me, and tell him I'll talk to him tomorrow."

"I will," Shannon promised.

Natalie hung up the phone, feeling more lost and alone than ever. When the tears came this time, she couldn't blink them away.

Another Friday night. Another weekend on the horizon. And Dylan was, as usual, alone. He left the police station, glanced across the parking lot at Natalie's office. It was in darkness.

Of course—Friday night, he reminded himself. She was in the habit of spending her weekends in Chicago, although he didn't know why. There were still far too many things he didn't know about the woman who preoccupied his thoughts, and it wasn't for lack of trying.

He'd made some inquiries—tactful and discreet, of course—through a friend of a friend who worked with the Chicago P.D. He'd learned that despite her work as a criminal defense attorney, even the local prosecutors and police spoke positively about her. She worked hard and played fair, and she was generally liked and well-respected.

Which would have been helpful if he was interviewing

her for a job. But he'd hoped for something more, something that would provide insight into her reasons for leaving Chicago. Something that might shed light on the mystery of her appearance in Fairweather and finally end his preoccupation with her. Nothing had.

He went home, changed his clothes, rifled through his cupboards and tried not to think about her. He grabbed his jacket and his keys and headed over to the Sizzling Wok for some take-out Kung Pao chicken, and he thought of Natalie again. The restaurant was just a few blocks away from the Courtland Hotel, and as he was driving by, he noticed her car was there. Apparently she hadn't gone to Chicago this weekend.

So, twenty minutes later, he was standing in the brightly lit corridor of the hotel, take-out bag in hand. He knocked, waited. At last he heard the click of the lock being released, then the door was open and Natalie was standing in front of him.

He allowed himself a quick survey, from the work socks bunched around her ankles, past shapely calves, to faded red sweatpants that had been hacked off at the knees. Her gray T-shirt was oversized and untucked, her hair pulled away from her face in a haphazard ponytail. But it was her eyes, puffy and red-rimmed and still swimming with tears, that startled him even more than her careless attire.

"Obviously I've come at a bad time," he heard himself say inanely.

She offered a weak smile. "I've had better days."

Growing up with three sisters, Dylan had plenty of experience dealing with crying women, but Natalie's tears struck something inside him. He wanted nothing more than to put his arms around her and promise to make everything better, but he wasn't sure she would welcome his support. "Do you want to be alone?"

"Actually, I could really use some company right now."

She stepped away from the door so he could enter.

"I thought you might be working on the Merrick case," he told her, offering a convenient excuse for his appearance on her doorstep. "And I thought maybe I'd give you a hand."

"You don't have anything better to do on a Friday night?"

"Not really," he admitted.

"I was working earlier," she told him. "I was just thinking about taking a break for dinner."

He held up the paper sack. "Kung Pao chicken."

She managed another smile. "An offer I can't refuse."

He followed her into the kitchenette, set the bag of food on the counter. He took the plates from her hands and put them down, then took her hands. Her fingers were cold, and they trembled slightly.

"Do you want to talk about it?"

Her blue-green eyes filled again, but she shook her head. "No."

"Sometimes it helps to vent your feelings."

A hint of her usual fire flickered in her eyes. "I don't need a confidant, Lieutenant, just a distraction."

She wanted a distraction?

His mouth crushed down on hers.

Chapter 8

He expected she would protest his domineering behavior. Maybe he wanted her to. But she didn't try to pull away. She didn't push him away. Instead, she wound her arms around his neck and kissed him back for all she was worth.

Mouths melded, tongues clashed, desires warred. It was primitive, almost violent, and unrestrained.

Dylan had thought he was taking control. From the minute his lips met hers, he realized his mistake. Neither one of them was in command. Once released, passions too long buried couldn't be subdued.

Her response was as raw as his demand; her desire as impatient as his own. It wasn't just about sex, though his body was aching to join with hers. He hadn't thought of another woman since he'd met Natalie. And with each day that had passed since then, he wanted her more.

No, it wasn't just sex, it was intimacy he craved. He'd

been alone—and lonely—for so long. Without even trying, Natalie had changed that. From the moment their hands had clasped in formal introduction, he'd felt alive. More alive than he'd felt in years.

He'd fought it, for a lot of reasons. Because he felt disloyal to his wife, because he felt guilty that he could find joy in life when hers had been taken away from her, but mostly because he didn't want the feeling of vulnerability that inevitably came with opening up one's heart to another. He couldn't fight it any longer. He wasn't going to pretend any longer. He wanted Natalie, only Natalie.

He wanted to touch not just her body, but her heart and her soul. At the moment, however, he was pretty damn distracted by the soft, slender body pressed against his. He slid his hands beneath the hem of her T-shirt and encountered silky flesh. She was so incredibly soft, so perfect. His hands moved higher, to cup her breasts. Even through the satin barrier of her bra, she responded immediately to his touch. Her nipples pebbled, strained against the fabric. He stroked his thumbs over the tips, teasing, caressing.

He broke the kiss only long enough to tug the T-shirt over her head and toss it aside. The contrast of emerald-green satin against her pale creamy skin distracted his attention—just for a moment. He would never have guessed that the proper Natalie Vaughn wore such seductive lingerie. And although he might fully appreciate her choice of attire at another time, right now he wanted her naked.

He found the clasp at the front, slipped it open.

He could hear her breathing, quick, panting gasps that assured him she was as aroused as he. But she put her hands on his, as if to halt his progress. "Dylan, I don't think—"

He wasn't sure what she was going to say, but he was certain he didn't want to hear it. Anything that contained the word *don't* didn't bode well for his immediate plans.

"Don't think," he interrupted, and silenced any further protest with his lips on hers. "Just feel."

He skimmed his lips down the slender curve of her throat, and her head fell back in surrender. Her hands dropped away, leaving his to explore freely. He pushed the cups of her bra aside to cradle the fullness of her breasts in his palms. She quivered in response to his touch, and Dylan felt his erection throb painfully inside his jeans. But he ignored his own discomfort and concentrated on Natalie.

Natalie—so soft and fragrant and so incredibly responsive. Her instinctive movements and whimpers of pleasure were driving him to the brink. He lowered his head and circled the peak of one nipple with his tongue. Her fingers were in his hair, holding him against her breast, encouraging his continued ministrations. He was determined not to disappoint her. He took the tip of her breast in his mouth and suckled deeply.

She gasped. "Oh—Dylan—no—please."

He could spend hours kissing her, caressing her. He loved the way she moaned and writhed. Her responses were so natural and uninhibited. And although he was quickly approaching the point of no return, he needed to know exactly what it was that she wanted. He raised his head reluctantly until his face was level with hers.

Her cheeks were flushed, her eyes clouded with passion. But he wasn't going to let there be any misunderstandings about what was happening. Not at this point in the game. "Which is it, Natalie? No...or please?"

"Please." There was no hesitation in her response.

He slid a hand over the gentle curve of her belly, slipped it inside the waistband of her sweatpants, into her panties, and found her slick and hot and ready.

This time it was Dylan who groaned.

Scooping her into his arms, he carried her the short distance across the room to the bed. He laid her down on top of the covers and knelt astride her partially naked body, then tugged her sweatpants over her hips, slowly sliding them down her legs. She had incredible legs, slender but toned and miles long. Her panties did, indeed, match the bra he'd already disposed of. They dipped low in the front and were cut high on the hips. They were sexy and provocative, and right now, they were in the way of what he wanted.

Before he could discard them, she grabbed him by the shirt and pulled him down on top of her. *She* kissed *him* this time, sliding her tongue into his mouth, teasing, tormenting. He tasted her impatience, her passion. Her hands were busy unfastening the buttons down the front of his shirt, then her palms were on his chest, sliding over his skin, stroking, seducing.

She pushed the fabric off his shoulders, then pulled him closer. Her breasts flattened beneath his chest; her hips arched against his. Even through his jeans, he could feel her welcoming heat, and he ached to be inside her.

"I want to make love with you, Natalie."

"You still have too many clothes on, Lieutenant."

He eased away from her. "Don't you think 'Lieutenant' is a little formal for the man who's about to get naked with you?"

Then he stripped away the last of their clothing and spread her thighs gently. Her natural scent enticed, seduced. He spread the soft folds of flesh to uncover the moist bud at her center and flicked his tongue over it. She cried out, her hips arching toward him in a movement that was completely instinctive, and utterly irresistible. He delved deeper, his tongue stroking her softness, savoring her juices.

Her breath was coming faster now, in quick shallow gasps. He felt the tension building inside her, coiling tight, tighter.

He increased his rhythm, plunging deeper, faster, until she finally shattered.

"Now, Dylan. Please." She was panting, quivering with the aftershocks of her release, and dripping with readiness.

He quickly sheathed himself with a condom, then finally slipped into the welcoming warmth between her thighs.

He wanted to bury himself in a single thrust, but she was tighter than he'd expected and he felt her tense again as he eased into her. So he forced himself to move slowly, sliding into her inch by inch. She gasped as he filled her, but she didn't hold back. She wrapped her legs around him, pulling him even deeper. He was encircled by her limbs, enveloped in her warmth, encompassed by her being. This was mating in the truest sense of the word: two separate people, joining together, becoming one.

Then he began to move inside her, and she matched him thrust for thrust in a synchronized rhythm that quickly brought Natalie to the brink of pleasure again, and sent Dylan tumbling over the edge with her.

Natalie wasn't in the habit of sharing intimacies with a man—her body or her bed. It had been seven years since she'd succumbed to the draw of passion. Until tonight, she hadn't even been tempted.

From the moment her body had joined with Dylan's she'd known it was a mistake, because somewhere in the midst of their union, she'd realized that she could fall in love with him. She wouldn't let that happen.

Her primary concern was, and always had been, her son, which left her little time or inclination for other emotional entanglements. She'd made that choice years ago. She didn't regret it then, she didn't regret it now. If she had any regrets at all, it was only that she'd made love with Dylan without having told him about Jack.

Deception wasn't something she was comfortable with, and although she hadn't intentionally deceived him, her silence about her child was dishonest and unfair. Or maybe she was being presumptuous. After all, Dylan had never given her any indication that he wanted anything more from her than what they'd just shared: sex. Incredible, mind-boggling, body-numbing sex, but still just sex.

The thought fizzled as his lips brushed the back of her neck.

"You awake?" His voice was low and husky with sleep.

"I'm awake," she admitted.

"Good." He slid away far enough to turn her onto her back, then he covered her mouth with his.

It started out as a leisurely kiss—slow and lazy. She didn't know who deepened the kiss, only that the tenor of it quickly changed. Breaths mingled, tongues tangled.

His hands were on her breasts now, caressing, enticing. He seemed to know just where to touch her, exactly what to do to give her the greatest pleasure. He lowered his head and laved one already erect nipple with his tongue. She closed her eyes and moaned as heat arrowed from that aching peak to her center. His mouth continued its sensual torture. His tongue flicked over the aching bud, his teeth nipped, and when he fastened his lips over the peak and suckled, she had to bite down on her lip to keep from crying out.

He moved from one breast to the other, ministering the same careful attention. She dug her heels into the mattress and lifted her hips, rocking against the solid length of his shaft. The friction of her movements alone nearly undid her. But that wasn't what she wanted. She wanted to feel him inside her.

She reached between their bodies and wrapped her fingers around his erection. She felt the organ pulse in her hand as she rubbed her thumb over the bead of moisture at the tip.

He groaned and captured her wrist, raising her hand above her head.

"I want to touch you," she told him.

"Not right now," he said. "I want you so much I'm almost ready to explode."

"Then take me."

"I will," he promised.

But first he made his way down the length of her torso, caressing her with his hands, his lips, his body, eliciting sighs and gasps and moans of pleasure from her. He drove her slowly, relentlessly, to the peak. When her climax ripped through her, he finally slipped inside, filling and fulfilling her.

Dylan hadn't planned to spend the night. But when the first rays of light started to filter into the room, he was still in Natalie's bed. His arm was around her middle, her back flush against his front.

Over the past several years, he'd looked forward to the middle of the night interruptions that were an inherent part of his occupation—anything to excuse the fact that he wasn't sleeping. But he'd slept last night, peacefully, contentedly, deeply.

It was the first time he'd spent an entire night with a woman since Beth died. It was an intimacy he'd never allowed himself, an intimacy he'd never wanted.

Last night, with Natalie, something had changed. He hadn't thought he'd ever want another relationship. He wasn't sure he could ever get over losing Beth. He'd loved her for so long, and when she'd died, a part of him had died with her.

Natalie made him feel alive again. She made him want to open his heart and share his life. As he watched her sleep, listened to the soft, even sound of her breathing, he knew he was in over his head.

It was supposed to have been just sex—a purely physical

act between two consenting adults. Somehow, it had become more, and he didn't have the slightest idea what to do about it. He didn't know how to handle this morning after, to answer the questions she was sure to ask.

It was this not knowing that unnerved him the most. He was accustomed to setting his own path, to being in control every step of the way. Natalie had changed all of that.

He started to shift away from her, knowing he needed some physical distance if he was going to put things into perspective. She turned her head, and he could smell the fruity scent of her hair.

He hesitated, torn between the need to escape and the desire to join his body with hers again.

Her eyelids fluttered, opened. "Dylan?"

He smiled, despite the tension knotted in his belly. "Good morning."

This time, he was certain she blushed, the soft light of the morning sun highlighting the spots of color. He traced a fingertip over her cheek, couldn't resist teasing her a little. "You seem surprised to see me."

She looked away, pulled the sheet a little higher, as if he hadn't already seen and touched every inch of her body. "Not surprised, it's just…um…"

Her uneasiness was oddly reassuring, a sign that she, too, had been affected by what transpired between them. "I wouldn't have stayed if I'd known it would make you uncomfortable."

"I just don't have a lot of experience with this sort of thing," she admitted.

And that admission brought to mind a dozen questions he knew he had no right to ask. Like "how much experience?" and "what exactly *is* this thing between us?"

But before he could respond, the shrill beep of his pager broke the silence.

"Sorry, I—"

She shook her head, dismissing his apology. "It's okay."

He slid out of the bed, digging through his clothes for the source of the intrusion. He found the offending instrument under his jeans and silenced the beep.

Scrubbing a hand over his jaw, he squinted at the digital message. And swore.

"What is it?"

"I have to go."

She nodded.

He disappeared into the adjoining bath to wash up and tug on his clothes. When he returned to the bedroom, she, too, was dressed. He wanted to kiss her goodbye, he wanted to hold her—to hold on to what they'd shared in the darkness of the night. It was the depth of this need that propelled him toward the door instead with a vague "I'll call you" tossed back over his shoulder.

He disregarded the speed limit as he drove across town, his thoughts again on Natalie, instead of the crisis that had summoned him from her bed.

He turned on to Osgood Street, the presence of a cruiser in the drive of number fourteen jolting him back to the present like the cool rain that had started to fall.

He parked on the road, in front of the house, and jogged up the walk of Victor Jennings's home. Jennings was one of the key witnesses in the case against Ellis Todd, and Dylan knew that whatever had happened here was somehow related to Roger Merrick's murder investigation.

Eriksson and Whittaker were the officers who'd taken the call; Eriksson met him at the door.

"What happened?" Dylan demanded, following the uniformed officer down the narrow hallway and into the kitchen.

"Mr. Jennings woke up this morning, came downstairs to

make a pot of coffee and read the newspaper. When he opened up the paper, he found a dead rat in it."

"I take it the rat didn't die of natural causes."

Eriksson grinned. "I guess that's why you're the lieutenant."

He waited, with obvious impatience, for the young officer to continue his explanation.

"It didn't die of natural causes," Eriksson confirmed. "The rat's throat had been slit across, so deeply it was almost decapitated."

The visual that came to mind wasn't pretty, but he'd seen a lot worse. "Any of the neighbors see anything?"

"We called in Jones and Lawford. They're canvassing the street right now. According to Mr. Jennings, who was barely coherent when we got here, the paper is delivered between five forty-five and six-fifteen every morning. That's a narrow window of opportunity."

"Maybe it was the paperboy," he suggested.

"Nah. We've already talked to the kid. Showed him the rat. He tossed his Frosted Flakes all over Whittaker's shoes."

Dylan allowed himself a small smile. He'd learned a long time ago to find humor in little things, otherwise the job would kill you. "I want to talk to the kid."

"Stephen Miller. Eleven years old. Sixth-grade student at Chappel Hill Middle School, lives a couple of streets over. The address is in the report."

He nodded and followed Eriksson into the kitchen.

Victor Jennings was seated at the kitchen table, still wearing his bathrobe, a mug of coffee—apparently untouched—held between his palms.

Dylan started to approach him, paused when he saw Whittaker come in through the back door, his coat and hat dripping rain.

"Neighbor saw a white Cadillac," Whittaker told him.

"Older model, tinted windows. Lots of rust, damaged muffler, Kansas plates. He said it was driving slowly, just before six o'clock this morning."

Dylan wouldn't have thought it was possible, but Jennings's face went even whiter. "Kansas?"

"Do you know someone in Kansas?" he asked.

"My wife's parents." Jennings swallowed. "My wife and daughters are visiting them right now."

He felt his skin grow cold. "Do your in-laws have a white Caddy?"

"They s-sold it."

"When?"

"I—I'm not sure. A few days, maybe a week ago."

About the same time that the witness list for the Ellis Todd trial was released to the defense. Dylan knew it wasn't a coincidence.

"Did the witness get the plate number?" he asked his officer.

Whittaker shook his head.

"Keep canvassing," he instructed. "Maybe someone else did."

He waited until Whittaker had left the house again before turning back to Jennings. "Call your wife," he instructed, gesturing to the phone on the wall. "I want to know exactly when her parents sold that car and who they sold it to."

"You think it was the same car?" Eriksson asked, his voice pitched low enough that only Dylan could hear.

Dylan was watching Jennings, whose finger was trembling so badly he could barely punch the numbers. He misdialed twice before completing the call.

"I'd bet on it," he finally replied to the question.

"And you think this all goes back to Conroy."

"I'd bet on that, too," he said grimly.

A hell of a lot of premeditation had been put into something that might otherwise have been dismissed as a childish prank. The vehicle had driven slowly down the street, had probably done so several times, with a muffler obviously in need of replacing. Whoever had been driving the vehicle had wanted to draw attention to it, had wanted it to be made.

Why?

Because Conroy wanted them to know it was him. This was his way of thumbing his nose at the authorities. Dylan had believed that he could get to Conroy by convicting Ellis Todd. With the help of one dead rodent, Conroy had demonstrated how unlikely that scenario was.

"This is all about that Todd case, isn't it?" Jennings asked, after he'd hung up the phone.

"It would be premature to draw any conclusions at this point," Dylan told him.

"Don't give me that crap," Jennings snapped. "I want to know if I'm in danger. If my family's in danger."

"We're not going to disregard the possibility," he said. "If we think there's any risk, we'll see that you're protected."

Jennings shook his head. "I never should have agreed to testify. I didn't even see anything."

"You saw Ellis Todd in Merrick's apartment building."

"I was on my way out of the building after visiting my cousin. Yeah, I saw that Todd guy coming in, but I didn't see him with the dead guy and I didn't hear any gunshots. Why do you need me?"

"You're the only one who can place the defendant at the scene of the crime. If you don't testify, a man may get away with murder."

"I don't care," Jennings said. "I don't know the killer or the man who was killed. I was just in the wrong place at the wrong time, and now my life—and the lives of my family—may be in danger."

"I understand that you're upset, Mr. Jennings, but—"

"You don't understand nothing," he interrupted. "You didn't find that mangled carcass on your doorstep."

"The police are doing everything they can to find out who put the rat there."

"Tell them to find another witness for your murder trial," Jennings advised. "Because I'm not setting foot in court."

Natalie was working in her hotel room, finishing her list of case law when she was summoned by a knock at the door. *Dylan,* she thought immediately, and chided herself when her heart skipped a beat. But she couldn't prevent the smile that curved her lips when she opened the door and found him standing in the hall.

"We've got a problem." His tone was cool, his gaze even cooler.

Her easy smile faded. Well, what had she expected—that just because he'd had sex with her it meant he cared? Unfortunately, that *was* what she'd expected. But the grim face of the man standing outside her door bore no resemblance to the tender, passionate lover who'd spent last night with her.

"Did you want to come in?" she asked, forcing her voice to remain carefully neutral.

He looked past her into the room, at the bed where they'd made love through most of last night. "I don't think that's a good idea."

That was certainly clear enough. She ignored the hurt, the disappointment. "What happened?"

"Victor Jennings is refusing to testify at the prelim."

"Why?"

"Because of Conroy." He practically spat the name out.

"What did he do?"

"He messed with his head."

"Tampering with a witness—"

"He wasn't obvious about it," Dylan interrupted. "That isn't his style. He sent an anonymous warning—in the form of a dead rat."

Her stomach churned as she listened to his recital of the incident. People like Zane Conroy were the reason she'd left Chicago. She'd wanted to escape from the craziness of the city, to protect her child from the big bad world. But she'd chosen Fairweather as her home, and she was determined to make it safe for her son. If Dylan could bring her the evidence tying this incident back to Conroy, she'd make damn sure Conroy was held responsible.

"Are you going to arrest Todd for obstruction of justice?" she asked.

Dylan scrubbed a hand over his face. His eyes were shadowed with fatigue, his mouth drawn tight with worry. There was a part of her that wanted to reach out, to offer comfort. But she knew it would be refused, and she wasn't prepared for that kind of rejection. After all that they'd shared the night before, she couldn't stand for him to turn away from her now.

"We could charge him," he agreed. "But what good will it do when we've lost a key witness on the original charge?"

"Jennings was subpoenaed," she told him. "He has to appear."

His laugh was harsh. "You think that's going to make a difference? Christ, Natalie, how naive are you?"

She could understand that he was upset; she couldn't understand why he'd made his attack personal. And she was hurt and angry enough by his attitude to fight back. "Don't get pissed off at me because of this. I didn't send him the damn rat."

"I'm pissed off at myself," he admitted.

"Why?"

"Because I should have anticipated that Conroy would engineer a stunt like this."

"What could you have done to prevent it?"

"I could have had Jennings under surveillance."

"Why him and not one of the others? There are several independent witnesses in this case. If it hadn't been Jennings, it would have been someone else." Instinct momentarily overruled common sense, and she reached out to lay a comforting hand on his arm. "It wasn't your fault."

"Wasn't it?"

The anger and disgust in his tone alerted her that there was something more going on than just his frustration with the case. She dropped her hand away, folded her arms across her chest. "What are you really angry about, Dylan? The fact that Conroy got to a witness? Or the fact that you were sleeping with me when it happened?"

"Both."

She'd known it was a mistake to get involved with him—for so many reasons. She'd known that what happened between them couldn't last. But to hear him so easily disregard their night together was more than she could take right now.

"I didn't invite you to come here last night," she reminded him. "You showed up on your own initiative with your Kung Pao Chicken and your damn dimples and now you're blaming me for what happened?"

"I didn't come here with the intention of making love with you."

"And when you said, 'Let me make love with you, Natalie'—what did you really mean? Pass the fried rice?"

"I know I made the first move," he admitted grudgingly.

"You made *all* the moves."

"You wanted me as much as I wanted you."

"I did," she agreed coolly. "My mistake."

She went back into her room and closed and locked the door behind her.